THE
CLASSROOM
AROUND
THE CORNER

THE
CLASSROOM
AROUND
THE CORNER

Lupe Padilla

MILL CITY PRESS

Mill City Press, Inc.
555 Winderley Pl, Suite 225
Maitland, FL 32751
407.339.4217
www.millcitypress.net

© 2024 by Lupe Padilla

Paperback ISBN-13: 978-1-66289-677-4
eBook ISBN-13: 978-1-66289-678-1

CONTENTS

INTRODUCTION

HELLO, YOU DON'T know me and depending on who you ask, you will receive many different names such as; spoiled brat, ungrateful, funny, creative, kind, scandalous, mischievous, and even dead. Who killed me you may be wondering, well that is the mystery in itself now isn't it. I will list off my suspects and by the end of the story let's see if you guessed correctly. Suspect number one is my best friend Deni. She has always been there for me. She knows every dark and dirty secret about me, the only one I could ever truly trust, until now. Suspect number two is my lustful lover, Cypher. The moment I laid eyes on him he enriched me into a whole new world through deception and lies luring me into a pit I could not get out of. Last, but not least, suspect number three is my very own mother who bore me in her womb giving me life and air to breathe raising me to the best of her ability and yet she hasn't looked for me while I am in this dark hole trying to catch my last breath.

Chapter ONE

"PAULINA HURRY UP! We are going to be late on our first day," said Deni.

"Okay, I am coming you know I have to have the right look," I responded back.

"Ugh, girl you are beautiful, just throw on your usual hoodie and jeans and wrap up your hair and call it good because you will not try anything else."

I come running out of my room frantically looking for my glasses and as I am scrambling through my backpack I see Deni holding up my glasses, "Looking for these?" she asks with a joker grin on her face.

"Give me that," I snatched them out of her hands. "Let's go, I am finally ready, how do I look?"

"Oh yeah, like a real party, woot woot!"

"Oh stop with the sarcasm, let's go!"

It is the first day of college. My excitement is making it hard to keep down my breakfast, it wasn't much; just three eggs, five bacon strips, two bananas, four waffles and a protein bar. Okay I admit this was more than I usually eat for breakfast, a lot more. I would normally just grab a protein bar and go on my way, but I can't help it. I am living with my best friend Deni away from the campus. We live in another state miles away from my mother. We are from a small town; Cortez, Colorado and we both got accepted to Georgetown. The craziest thing I have ever done was to leave home. I tried being the perfect daughter as long as I could remember, deep down I always knew I could never truly measure up to the high expectation of my mother's standards.

"Girl, are you not pumped, this is our first day of college and soon you will be the greatest psychologist that ever healed these streets!" Deni blurted out.

"Haha, yeah! Can't forget you will be the best business woman negotiating and persuading an eskimo to buy ice," I replied.

As we pull up to the parking lot I swallow hard, digging through my backpack to find my schedule. As you suspect, my schedule is not even here. I throw my backpack to the ground in complete frustration.

"Paulina, are you okay? What's wrong?" she asks me with a look of complete concern on her face.

"No, Deni, I am not okay. I can't find my schedule and I don't know where my classes are or even what time they start."

"Hey, look at me. It is okay, you can go to the administrative office and request a new one."

"Okay, you are right, let's go." I say completely at ease.

"Well you will have to go by yourself, my class starts literally in 10 minutes and I have to go find it. Love you tons!"

Before I could even reply back she already got out of the car and started going towards the entrance doors. Well looks like I am meant to take this journey alone. As I struggle to open the car door, I take a deep breath and count to three. If I didn't do it at that moment I knew I wouldn't ever leave the car. I walk out and shut the door, placing my backpack over my shoulder. Heading towards the entrance door anxious to get to the other side, oh how my life would change forever from this first step. Little did I know it would be the first step to the plot of my death. Thankfully the administrative office was easy to find. I don't think I could handle any more pressure of roaming around feeling lost.

"Hello, excuse me, can anyone help me?" I ring the front desk bell. Feeling even more anxious and frustrated. "Please can anyone help me? Is anyone there?" I feel a cold shiver going down my back, an intensity that you only get when ice is rubbing against your skin. A thousand different sensations hitting every nerve in my body. Why does this feel more like a warning? As I close my eyes to take in the moment...

"Hello," a strange young woman spoke. Scaring me out of that moment. My mouth is dry and I am terrifyingly speechless. "How can I help you?" she asks politely as can be and yet still impatient.

"Um, yes. I am here to get another schedule if I can please, I accidentally misplaced my old one and I really need to get another one because I am pretty sure my first class is about to start in the next 15 minutes and I am really freaking out as it is..."

"Hey, calm down. I don't need your whole life story because I am believing that is where it is headed. Look, tell me your name and I will print you off another one."

"Oh, okay, um Paulina; Paulina Saville," she turns her face towards the computer screen typing in my name. My hand couldn't help but tap away on the counter top as if I were sending a morris code letting everyone know that I need to get out of here pronto!

"Well here you go, P.S." she says while giving me this piece of paper.

"Thank you so much, uh Joselyn." Hesitantly reading her name tag, I moved away from the front desk with my schedule in my hand walking towards the doors as I realized how she said my name, I began to turn around to ask her why she called me P.S. but she was gone.

I shrug it off and look down at my schedule. To my surprise I saw a class there that I have never seen. Of course it would be my first class that is literally starting in 5 minutes. I had no time to spare to talk about this class, maybe it is added on because it is a required class that I never realized I needed to take. Maybe they are being considerate because I overlooked some prerequisites for this year. At this point I am desperately running through the halls to find room 236. Through my chaotic running I end up bumping into a woman and falling to the ground. She was tall and beautiful, and could have easily been a runway model with her long red hair, skin as milk and gorgeous green eyes. She is standing in complete confidence, unfazed about what just happened.

"Here let me help you up," she says so genuinely. As she reaches for my hand with such a warm and welcoming smile.

"Thank you, I am so sorry I didn't mean to run into you. It is my first day and I am trying to find this room that was sprung on me at the last minute and I am so lost and I..."

"Calm down," she grabs my face. "Look, take a few deep breaths with me. Breathe in and breathe out, breathe in and breathe out." She is just staring into my eyes as if she is trying to figure me out, I pull away from her and her hand drops. "How do you feel?"

"Much better thank you for asking."

"Here maybe I can help, what class are you looking for?"

"Room 236, do you know where that is or even what that is. It says The Connection Between Art and Psychology. I have never heard that before."

"Yes, I know where that is. I am actually headed there myself. It's definitely a difficult class to pass. I will let you in on a secret. I am retaking this class because I have failed."

"Oh, I am sorry to hear that."

"It's no biggie, the moment you enter the classroom you will see why it is so easy to be distracted and wouldn't mind repeating the course. My name is Ansa. What is yours?"

"My name is Paulina"

"Hmm, I am going to call you Lina. Let's get you to class. We wouldn't want you to be late on your first day, thankfully we are almost there."

As I follow alongside her I can feel her eyes staring at my outfit of choice and smiling. It almost felt as if she was judging me, but more so she was making me feel like innocence was a prize to be won. We are completely down the hall. I see no classroom in sight. I question the fact if she was even someone I should be trusting.

"Here we are!" She points to a classroom, hidden around the corner.

I pull open the classroom door and I see everyone turn their heads to me. I swallowed so hard that a log must have gotten stuck in my throat because I couldn't help but cough severely soon after, making it hard to breathe.

"Are you okay?" Ansa asks me while giving me a hard pat on my back. I gave her a nod as I was catching my breath. I am sure everyone heard how I was struggling to get myself together at this point because as I looked up I saw them still all glaring at me through my watery eyes. Whispers were so loud that I could hear my ears ringing. I wanted to believe it was because I was 32 seconds late coming into the door. But the truth was likely because I looked like a fish out of water trying to flop its way back in. Ansa must have seen my cheeks quickly turn red because the next thing I knew she was waving me over to a seat next to her. How did she get over there so quickly? I started making my way through the seats to get to her trying to keep my head as low as possible as if I didn't cause enough attention to be set on me. Not even if I was a chameleon could hide me from their eyes. The only reason I was no longer the center of the attention was because there was a noise coming from the corner of the classroom. As I took my seat and reached for my notebook and pencil, I was able to successfully place the notebook on my desk but my clumsy self was still so nervous from what just happened that I completely missed placing my pencil on my desk and the floor decided to say, "Yeah, I'm here too. Thank you for noticing."

"Ugh, you have to be kidding me," as I reach to pick up my pencill, I clash with someone else's hand. As I slowly look up from his massive hands, to his arms truly complementing his button up shirt, I see a smile with the most perfect and whitest teeth, his eyes emerald green, his skin smooth like butter and his hair perfectly cut and styled that all I could say was, "How perfect is a massive shirt."

Before I could even slump in my shame and hide forever he simply said, "You're welcome," with the most charming smile giving me back my pencil and walked away.

I look at Ansa redder than a rose. "Do you know who that is?"

"Oh yeah that is…"

"Hello everyone, my name is Professor Cypher Williams, but you can call me Cypher."

Wow, why did I have to become a cliche and develop intimate urges for my professor. I was completely blind sided. Go figure.

Chapter TWO

"HERE I WANT to show you something," he said so effortlessly, grabbing my arms leading me into a room that was unfamiliar. As I slowly walk into the room I remove myself from his arms as I am captivated by the artwork in this room. I came across the details of this piece that shows two beings as close as they can possibly be, oh how it would be a crime waiting to be charged if they were ever to be apart. The passion and flame in their facial expression tells every pain and pleasure they had together. As I am mesmerized by the painting I can also hear every "I love you" being replaced with a groan, every ``I need you" with a moan. I then hear a door slam and lock behind me, he is leaning up against the door with his arms folded. Staring down at me as if he is trying to observe my every move. Every muscle in his jaw, chest, and arms began to tighten; I started to slowly walk over to him. My arms grabbing the back of his neck, I look into his eyes that seemed to be an endless story and lean in to kiss him, my chest up against his. Then, what happened next happened so fast, he grabs my waist and picks me up and walks over to the bed still harmonizing with my tongue and throws me on the bed. I look up and he crawls on the bed like a hungry lion, ready to attack its prey and starts kissing me again and begins to trail down to my neck then up to my ear whispering; "Paulina, when are you going to wake up." After saying that he slides back looking down on me as if he was mocking me.

"Excuse me," I say with such confusion.

"Paulina!" he yells as he reaches to grab after me. I start punching my way through as I wake up.

"Hey! Hey! Paulina calm down it's just me," Deni says as she is grabbing my wrists so I don't end up punching her in the face.

"What, oh my, what just happened?"

"Honey, you fell asleep while I went to get some dinner for us."

"Oh, I am so sorry I was writing my paper on the mental state of the artist on this painting and I must have passed out."

"Yeah, I bet you were writing about the artist. I would have been bored too when I can just dream about some sexy professor."

"Oh stop it, who said I was even dreaming about Cypher?"

"I never said anything about Cypher. I could have been talking about Professor Higgens. Plus honey you know how to make a pro blush with all the sounds coming out of your mouth. Cypher must have liked it really rough if he has you swinging out of your sleep, darling next time establish a safeword."

"Wow, only you. I am not having this conversation with you. What did you get?"

"Don't hate the player, hate the game. I got us Chinese, here." She hands me my chopsticks and orange chicken that I truly enjoy.

Now as the update goes on Professor Cypher, I have been in his class for a month now and every night is the same. Showing up in my dreams seducing me. Being in his class is not easy, the way he talks and winks at me when no one is looking, which seems often, makes me want to forget anyone really is even there. Everytime we have to turn in a paper he tells me to stay behind so he can praise me for the work I've done and then completely degrades me when it still doesn't meet his requirements. Such a double minded man and yet I am completely intrigued at the game of chess he is playing.

"Thank you, for going to get us food can you please pass the soy sauce"

"Here you go."

The room grows quiet. I look at Deni practically begging her to drop the conversation and move on, to literally talk about anything else; shoot Einstein's Relativity Theory would be a lot less stressful to break down than talking about how I can't stop thinking about the professor. In this weird way this whole situation is like gravity, the more weight of how much I want to have him the faster my understanding of such an intimacy is continuously curving, practically pulling me into an infinite black hole that I dare to explore. Knowing Deni she is not the one to let it go, better yet she would give me a million reasons why I should fall into my urge as if she is trying to persuade me to buy into the whole sexual experience.

"Girl, screw him already!"

"Why am I not surprised that you wouldn't let it go."

"Because I love you too much, plus what are you holding out for, you are really quite the catch with your milk chocolate skin, golden brown eyes, and long wavy onyx hair. If I am not mistaken you said that he may even possibly be into you, am I wrong?"

"I am not entirely sure I said that."

"You told me that when you guys have your quote on quote one on one time that he presses up against you, getting close to show you what is exactly wrong with your paper. More like what exactly are you missing out on, you know what I mean?." She starts laughing hysterically while dry humping the air.

I start laughing with her, "Oh my goodness, stop! Yeah I said that, I just don't want to assume, plus why do you ask me what I am waiting for? You haven't done anything yet."

"You are right I haven't done anything... yet. I don't plan on waiting though I am not like you trying to wait for marriage or something."

"What's wrong with that anyways, I wouldn't necessarily say I was waiting for marriage I just said I want to wait until that right one comes along and that I am in love with them."

"Love," she says with a scuff, "is that even real?"

"I don't know, but I would *love* to find out someday." We both give that goofy look at each other knowing what was intended and couldn't help but giggle.

"Here, I will go to your class tomorrow and I want to see Professor Cypher for myself. Unless for any reason I shouldn't go."

"You can come if you want, you might get bored sitting in that class, there is nothing you would be interested to learn about."

"You are right, art is more your thing, but I will be observing a specific piece of *art*," she says while winking and smirking at me.

"Oh, stop it," I push her while giggling. "Thank you for the food again, I am going to finish my work and go back to sleep, I need to wake up early and hit the library to check out another book."

"You're welcome, okay goodnight see you tomorrow."

Beep! Beep! Beep! Ugh, could alarms be any more annoying? Yes, don't judge me. I know the point of an alarm, I just wish there was a different tactic of waking me up instead of scaring me to death.

"Paulina! Turn off that dang alarm, I get it, I am awake too, thank you for that!"

"Ugh! Okay!" I reached for my alarm clock and turned it off. I roll over pulling the covers over my head. I know I need to get up, but I am struggling. Every waking moment he is on my mind and everytime I close my eyes he is there. Maybe I should take Deni's advice and push things further with him, just test the boundaries. I finally roll out of my bed and get into the shower. As the heat is touching my skin, I remember the heat of his touch rubbing my shoulders and grabbing my waist; I never told Deni because I know she

would freak if I told her I ended up running away. I step out of the shower and finish getting ready, I head into the kitchen and grab my orange juice and protein bar.

"Good morning sleeping beauty, how did you sleep?" I say as Deni comes into the kitchen looking like a zombie fresh from the grave..

"Ah ha, very funny. You clearly can see that I slept like crap. Go ahead to the library without me. I need extra time to get my look together, meet me at the student center and we can walk down to your class together."

"I was hoping you would forget or be too tired to even come."

"Oh no I wouldn't miss meeting him," she says smiling while biting into an apple.

Great, am I ready for her to meet Cypher, am I ready for any slick comment that may come out of her mouth while in class? The answer if you haven't guessed it yet is, no.

As I am looking at my watch, I notice how the seconds keep moving forward; stopping for no one, not even reversing to change any situation or even a conversation. My heart sinks to my stomach turning inside just like the wheels of a clock. To be even more specific every thought is like the harmonic oscillator in a clock, it is what keeps the frequency of the pendulum of my nerves to allow regret to keep turning in the hands of time. As I am searching through the library isles to look for books about art, I happen to stop at this one book that is called, Kama Sutra. As I reach towards the book out of curiosity, I hear a big bang behind me that makes me jump. Turning around I see Dillon, who is a classmate in Professor Cypher's class. I bend down to help him pick up the books he accidentally dropped.

"Here you go Dillon."

"Oh thank you, sorry for scaring you, I didn't mean to, I was just reaching for another book."

"That's okay, accidents happen. I see that you are collecting a lot of research for your paper that Professor Cypher assigned."

"Yeah, I am trying to pass his class. Almost seems impossible though."

"Here you go; last book," I say, stacking the book on top of the rest in his hands. "Do you need help with anything?"

"Paulina, if you can pass this class please tell me how you do it. I have retaken this class a few times and unfortunately I need to pass in order to get out of here. Whatever you do, don't fail; it will destroy you."

"Paulina!!!" I jump, hearing a voice coming from the other end of the aisle. I turn to look behind me and see Deni poking her head around the corner.

"Shhh... we are in a library," I say, trying to keep her voice down. I look back to continue my conversation with Dillon, but he already disappeared. It's okay I will see him in class and maybe then I could ask him what he meant and why he was so nervous, afraid even. What did he know that I hadn't seen yet?

"Let's go girl, I need to go see this fine professor of yours and see if he is worth the wet dreams you have been having."

"Shhh… okay fine I need to check out these books first." As I am walking towards Deni I remember the book that caught my attention and I turn back around to grab it, as I stand in front of the book shelf I didn't see it anywhere, it was gone, vanished even. Nothing but a blank space in between two books.

"Lina!! Come sit over here next to me and Zared."

"Come on Deni, I want you to meet a couple of my classmates."

"Well who is this tall glass of stylish sassy pants with you?"

"This is my best friend Deni, she wanted to come and observe my class today. She has been seeing how this class has been quiet… stressful and she just wants to see why. Isn't that right Deni?" I ask giving her a stern look to not spill my secret.

"Oh, yeah for sure. You guys are?"

"My name is Ansa and this is Zared. I like you Deni, you're very raw and rare. Enjoy the class. Hopefully we can see you back here soon. You are quite the catch." She says while glaring back at Zared with a smirk that didn't sit well with me, but I shrugged it off. My focus shifted so I could find Dillon.

"Settle down, settle down class, let's get started!" Cypher approaches the front of the classroom as if he was running the show, this man revealing dominance and power. Taking off his leather jacket as if he was trying to take off his own shackles, made me have a spot of sympathy for him.

"What!!" Deni yells in my ear. "You did not tell me he was that sexy!!"

I quickly snapped my neck to turn to Deni, staring her down into her bright blue eyes., "Girl shut up, everyone can hear you." I whisper in her ear feeling my face turning red.

"Honey, I don't care if they hear me, with a man like that I want people to hear me, you know what I mean? Now I see why you can't stop having those dreams, shoot if you don't make it a reality soon I will and I'll let you know how it is."

"Be quiet!" I say even louder looking at her with such worry.

"Mhmm," clearing his throat right in front of us. "Who may you be?"

"My name is Deni, sir. I am sorry I didn't mean to interrupt your class, please continue with your lecture." she turns to me and whispers, "Yes so I may learn a thing or two." I look at her and she winks.

As he turns around and continues to teach the lesson. I turn to Deni and see her ready to pounce him at any moment's notice. What have I done? Would my best friend really sleep with the professor? Do I have to claim him first in order for girl code to kick in? I could hardly pay attention to the lecture because my mind was all about the what if's that could possibly take place between Deni and Cypher. Am I starting to get jealous, is there rage starting to boil up within me against my bestfriend, the only one I truly considered family.

"Well, that wraps up for today. Don't forget your assignments are due next friday on the topic about the perspective of art," as I am packing up my things as quickly as I could getting ready to book it out of the classroom undetected so I could... "Paulina, may I see you for a moment?"

"Oh no," I whisper under my breath. I turn around to see Cypher sitting at his desk, I give him a simple reply, "Yes, sir." I am scared out of my mind, mainly because of how embarrassed I am feeling from the incident that happened earlier. I look at Deni and say, "Hey, I'll meet you at the cafe. You know what I like, I won't be long."

"Okay, I'll go catch up with Ansa and Zared. They seem pretty nice, we will meet you there."

"Okay, fine."

As she walks out, the door behind her closes and my legs begin to shake as I slowly walk down the stairs that seem to be miles long. "Yes, Professor Cypher."

"What was that stunt pulled in class today?" Those jaws of his clinching, his hand gripping around his red pen, and his eyes giving me a dagger look.

Shocked, embarrassed, and scared at what he just asked me, I couldn't help but play dumb and ask him, "What stunt? I don't know what you're talking about."

Slamming his paper on the desk, his head drops, jaw softens a bit and his hands are now clinging to the desk. Slowly looking up at me examining every inch of me he starts to walk over to me, his pecs leaning up against my chest. Staring me down he grabs my bag and tosses it to the floor. As I begin to look over to where he threw it, he grabs my cheek and starts kissing me aggressively and yet with complete passion. I couldn't find it in myself to push him away so I wrap my arms around him and start kissing him back. Our tongues are restoring lost time. As if we were fighting and making up. I can feel his arms wrap around me, his muscles securing himself against me and his hands engaging themselves on to my body. "Mmmm," he groans and picks me up. My legs wrapping around him not wanting to let go, he sits me on the desk pushing everything to the floor. I can't help but think of every filthy dream I've had about him and how much I am excited for this moment to finally be happening. As I lean back away from him, he starts to unbutton his shirt slowly, as I check out every muscle and vein popping out in his hands and arms. I get so weak and he knows it so he begins to climb on top of me hovering over my body like fog, his shoulders calling for me to pull him closer. We start kissing again and he starts kissing me on my neck using one hand to unbutton my blouse. The kisses begin to give me chills and I can feel myself getting turned on, a feeling I only dealt with in my recent dreams, he begins to kiss up to my earlobe and whispers in it saying, "You will be mine." I moan as these words flow down to my clitoris. "Your friend should mind her tongue before I have a better use for it," he says seductively. I push him off of me quickly. I start buttoning up my blouse.

"Why would you say that?"

"Well you guys being close friends and all I assumed you guys were in fact; close. Especially the way you let her talk about me, it was flattering really, even the way she was looking at me."

Completely broken about what he is telling me right now, I was hoping this was a dream, trying to pinch myself awake. I am shocked that such things are coming out of his mouth. I could feel water coming to my eyes like a sprinkler getting ready to go off. "Why are you even telling me this?" I finally got the guts to ask. "If you want to sleep with her then go ahead, but whatever just happened here, will not happen again!" I picked up my bag and headed to the door.

"Just like that, it's that easy. When's the last time you actually fought to get something first from her? When was the last time you didn't let her get what she wants?"

As I am focused on these questions I just shake my head and walk out heading to the cafe, I am debating on whether or not I should just go back to the apartment. As I am walking, I am reminiscing about the current events that took place, how amazing it was until he opened up his stupid mouth. How dare he talk about Deni, what would he want with her? She just came in for one day and I've been here for a month and he already wants to get in her pants too, seriously what gives? As I am thinking about everything my phone starts to ring, it's Deni. What does she want? Of course she gets everything she ever wanted. I have nothing to say to her right now, she should have never come into the classroom, I should have never let her go through those doors.

Chapter THREE

I AM RUSHING back to the classroom to go get my books I had left on my desk. I am by the door and hear a moan. I became very curious as to if I heard that sound correctly so I began to slowly open the door.

"Oh please keep going." It was dark. I could see there was a desk light shining on two figures that were hard to make out. As I creeped in to get a closer look I saw a male figure coming up between the young woman's legs and pulling her closer to him, his head is down so I can hardly get a good look. I walk even closer and the lady lays back and it is Deni! She is moaning to every thrust that, oh no, that can't be, Cypher is making! I am in complete shock and my heart is broken, he must have sensed my pain in the room because Cypher looks up at me and smiles, staring at me as if he wished it were me on that desk. Deni looks at me laughing hysterically as if she won. I try backing up to run away and Ansa and Zared grab me from behind.

"Can't you see he wants you to join Lina? Come join us, the pleasure is enticing no other feeling can measure up. Plus what more can you lose she already won..." Ansa says while mocking me. I turn around and see Cypher behind me and he pulls me down, I gasp for air.

I jump out of bed trying to catch my breath. What was that dream about? I turn over and see 5 missed calls from Deni and missed texts from Ansa and Zared. I then look at the time it is 3:00 a.m. Did I really just miss my other classes? I remember I came back home, took a shower to wash Cypher off of me, I told Deni that I wasn't feeling good and not to wait up for me at the cafe and then I started working on my paper. I guess I just passed out and missed dinner too, weird. I headed towards the kitchen to get some water. My throat was like the Sahara Desert after that dream, I felt so weak; that dream seemed to have drained me. As I entered into the kitchen...

"Paulina?"

"Deni, what are you doing up?"

"I just got in, what are you doing up?"

"I can't sleep, where are you coming from?" I ask hesitantly, was she coming in from screwing Cypher, hoping I didn't just dream about some sort of a reality.

"A party that Ansa and Zared invited me to, we were trying to reach you to see if you felt better to come out, but you never answered."

"Wait, you went to a party? Were you drinking?"

"Yes, I was drinking. What are you some sort of cop? I can experiment. We no longer live in a shelter life like we did back in Colorado. Isn't that what college is for, is to experiment, at least that's what everyone else says!" She declares while throwing her jacket and purse on the couch.

"I just asked you a simple question, I don't know why you are coming at me like this. I am going to guess you are probably drunk then, so I am going to go back into my room before any regrets come out of either of our mouths."

"That's your problem Paulina, everytime you come across something uncomfortable you hide in your room, that won't solve your problems. For once just go after something you want instead of letting other people get it first and you sit there with a victim mentality!" She says trying to hold herself up against the wall.

"Goodnight, Deni!" I go back into my room and slam my door. Where did that even come from? When does she drink? When does she just think that I have a victim mentality? Who is she to say those things to me? Fine, you want me to go after what I want, then I will get something you haven't experienced first and then you will see I am no longer a victim and will win the prize. I am going to have sex with Cypher!

*Ding, *Ding. My phone keeps receiving notifications. What time is it? I pick up my phone and see it, it says 9:23 am. Oh no! I missed my first class. I need to hurry and jump and get ready to make my other classes. As I am getting ready, I keep hearing my phone go off. Who can this be? I open up my phone and it is a message from Cypher! How did he get my number? What does he even have to say to me after what he said yesterday? I open the messages and they read as this:

Cypher: "Good morning sexy, I can't stop thinking about the amazing time we had, I wish you would have just let me do to you what I've been dying to do to you."

As I read those words, chills run up my spine, drawing me into curiosity of what else he has to say.

Cypher: "The way your lips taste so sweet, my very own addiction that leaves a trace like no other. How I want to feel your soft plum lips again. But next time I want them to be traced to somewhere else, if you catch my drift. ;)"

Cypher: "Don't make me wait another moment without you, every inch of your body was meant to be in my hands. My tongue was meant to engrave my name into every curve, while your nails do the same to my back."

I get so red and hot that I can't help myself. I begin to take my hand and trail down to a place I've never experienced for myself... *Ring, Ring, Ring! I jump up and answer the phone, "Hello."

"Are you touching yourself yet?" A seductive and intrigued voice says.

"Excuse me?"

"I know you read those messages, and I know you can't help finding yourself imagining me opening up your world to something you have never seen before. Go ahead, finish, I'm a good listener."

"Cypher, don't flatter yourself. How did you get my number anyways?"

"I have my ways."

"Well lose my number, I never gave it to you!"

"Oh but you did. The moment you let me kiss you, touch you. Even the moment you didn't allow me to escape your mind I was already given permission."

"Wh, wh, what?" Speechless, I had no response. Then I hear a light chuckle and click. How dare he say that and just hang up. I look down at my phone and see that it is already 10:15! How did time just pass me like that, I need to go. I have 30 minutes to get to my next class. I run out of my room and grab my backpack, as I pass the kitchen remembering what happened between Deni and I last night I just shrug. I look over to the living room and see her lying halfway on the couch and the rest of her on the floor, I guess she never made it to her room. As much as I wanted to leave her like that, I couldn't find it in my heart to do so. I pull her all the way on the couch and remove her shoes. I go to the nearby closet to get a blanket and cover her up. Then heading into the kitchen to get some water so I can place it on the table next to her, I go and search into her bathroom for any Aspirin. As I am digging through everything to find something, I come across a drawer that has condoms, a vibrator, and Kama Sutra. What was this book? I opened it up and there were pages filled with so many pictures of different sex positions.

Why was this turning me on? Why was this consuming me into a deep pleasure, allowing me to not look away. A quick dopamine of sensations tingling all over my body?

As I am sitting in my World History class I can't help but think about what I just saw in her drawer. Why would those things be in there? Has she already experienced sex before me? If so, with who? Could it be with Cypher, is that why he said what he said yesterday?

"Miss Paulina!"

"Yes, Professor Dana" I say hesitantly, coming out of my thought process.

"I asked you, what is the main reason history begins to repeat itself?"

"Oh, uhh," I am trying to regain my focus as I see her look growing impatient with me, "It is because we don't learn from previous experience. So therefore we are subjected to stay trapped in a cycle based on making the decision to not ever change our ways."

"Okay, follow up question. Do you think we would be able to allow history to stop repeating itself?"

"Well, as a whole, no. There is too much pressure to hold everyone accountable for their actions. I believe if we focus on trying not to repeat history in our own lives we can be accountable for ourselves. And through that we can slowly start to help others to break out of their own cycles. We may live in this world, but our own lives are the very world we need to conquer over."

"I like that perspective, as Shakespeare once quoted, 'All the world's a stage, and all the men and women merely players. They have their exits and their entrances; And one man in his time plays many parts.' Looking back to that and connecting it to what Paulina just said, we all have a part to play in overcoming certain obstacles in our lives to not allow history, whether our own or the history of those we love around us, to repeat itself. The goal of this world is the same; to stay in a cycle motivated by running off of brokenness. Trying to keep us focused on the lack of hope and faith certain circumstances can cause. Making us believe that there is no light at the end of the tunnel or even in the tunnel. There are many broken pieces within us, we should be obligated to see that we need help to break out of such dark history and instead make history not allowing ourselves to be consumed in the mentality that our trauma and lack of healing is okay." Her message seems to start resonating in me, I can't help being captivated by the lesson she is trying to teach us. Allowing me to believe there is truly something called hope out there. That it is not just a word but it can truly be tangible and obtained in my everyday life. That seeking out help is okay, even a courageous thing to do. "Okay class, that is heavy enough for today. Your end of the year assignment is simply this, I've never done this before but here it is, write about the history you possess, and a loved one possess, show what makes you become trapped in a cycle and what can we do to break that cycle off of not only our lives but also in the person we love. We should not only long for ourselves to flourish but to also help others flourish. Now since this will be a heavy evaluation, this will be your only assignment for this year and this paper will determine if you pass or fail. Now go enjoy your weekend, I will see you all next week." I quickly grab my things.

How am I supposed to know what part of the broken cycle I am in, how many broken parts could possibly be there in me? I begin to feel afraid, maybe I am too broken, that I am beyond repair, maybe I am not good enough for any restoration or redemption.

As I am entering the cafe, I notice Ansa, Zared, and Deni sitting down at a table, laughing amongst each other.

"Lina! Come join us!" Deni yells across the cafe.

"Hey, everyone! I am guessing they converted you to saying my nickname now."

"Haha, yes they did. I kind of like it. It is simple and cute. Just like you," she says smiling. There is something going on with her, she doesn't seem like the Deni I know. I don't know why the sudden change.

"Is that a bad thing?"

"Oh no, not at all. Deni just means that sometimes we need to get some complexity in your life, like going to this party with us. We will transform you from being cute to sexy!" Zared says with such enthusiasm.

"You are going to another party tonight? Did you go to any classes today, Deni?"

"Who are you, my mom? I only had one class today and I just got out. It's just a party, plus it is the weekend, live a little."

"Hey, Deni, come with me to go get our orders. What do you want, Lina?" Zared says, grabbing her by the arm to get up.

"I'll just take a small iced latte."

"You got it boss!" I began staring them down every step they took away from us. Why are they both being so weird? As my stare grows more intense I lose my focus when...

"Hey, Lina!" Ansa says to grab my attention. "Please come out with us, you don't have anything against partying, do you?"

"What? No! I just want to focus on my school work."

"Mmm, no I am not buying that. I am going to tell you what I think, and if I am right you have to come to the party, if I am wrong you don't have to, sound fair?"

43

"Fine, I'll play your game."

"Great! You like to stay so focused on school because you believe that is your one true form of success and control in your life. You believe if you work really hard you will receive praise and acknowledgement from your mother. Because of the lack of any attention from her you break your back to try everything to please her with how much you strain yourself to be perfect. With no dad in the picture you don't know the love of any genuine person. More proud, then humble you are. Your guard is up so high setting standards to things that can not ever be obtained. You love the attention you do get, that is why you place on a victim mentality because at least you are getting some attention, you play that game so well that you play others to a fault. Especially with Cypher, now am I right?"

My eyes lit up like a firework! "With Cypher, what are you talking about?"

"Oh, c'mon I saw the two of you," she says while giving me a wink as if she just defeated me. "I am going to assume that I am right, so we will be heading back to your place to get you ready for the party."

I have no words to say. I look away out towards the window. How can she possibly know any of those things, unless Deni told her. I turn around and I notice Ansa was walking over to the other two. As I was trying to see the conversation between Zared and Deni it seemed to be intense, I couldn't help but wonder what they could possibly be talking about? Ansa goes over and tells them something because all I could see was them smiling devilishly while looking at me as if they just plotted something, I begin to feel scared.

Clash!! Trays and two people fall to the ground.

"Oh no, I am so sorry. I shouldn't have turned so quickly, here let me help you," a small waitress spoke. She grabs the couple from the ground and leads them to the bathroom while a barista goes out to clean it up.

"Lina!" a slam on the table scares me out of my concentration.

"Hey, guys! Wait, how did you get on this side of me, I thought you guys were still in line over there?" I am confused.

"No, we were in that line over there getting our order, see." Deni says as she is pointing in the direction they just came from. They all grab their seats. "Here you go Lina one small iced latte."

"Thank you guys, what do I owe you?"

"No payment necessary," Zared says, flipping his brownish hair.

"Well at least for now," Ansa says laughing.

They all begin to laugh, "They are only joking, you will just owe them a shot later," Deni says trying to ease my mind.

"Oh," I say with a light giggle, "okay, I guess that will be okay." I swallow hard, I've never taken a shot before. Let's be honest, I have never drank before. How nerve wrecking is this. I take a sip of my drink and turn to Deni, "Hey, you and Zared seemed to have an intense conversation over there, are you guys okay?"

She looks into Zared's brown eyes, then back at me and starts to say, "Yeah, it was intense, the barista taking our order asked us what our major was and got us involved in a deep conversation trying to persuade us that psychology is a form of mind control. Of course I don't believe that; psychology is to help those with mental troubles and daily life troubles as is. Not basically hypnotizing us to believe something works, providing some sort of healing that temporarily comforts us and blinds us from what could actually heal us. Well what are your thoughts Lina?"

I didn't know what to think, that was too deep of a topic to explore and just hearing it, completely drained me mentally so I gave them an answer to get them off of me, "I will have to evaluate that topic a bit more, but as a psychology major I do believe there is truth in giving

47

advice to people for the better. I think the bigger question is, is it the right kind of advice being given that helps get them through their strongholds?"

"That is a good question." Deni says, shrugging at me with an attitude.

I wish that was the topic of their conversation. How do I know that, don't forget I am telling this story from a different time frame. But little did I know then, what was about to happen, was the next step leading to my death.

Chapter FOUR

LOUD MUSIC IS echoing off what seemed like every wall in this frat house. "Why did I make that deal with you Ansa?"

"Because deep down you want a taste of the underground!" She laughs uncontrollably.

"C'mon guys this way!" Zared yells at us to follow him through the crowd.

By the time I catch up, Deni hands me my first shot of the night. "Uh, I don't want one, thank you though."

"Girl, take it! Get loose, I promise you, you won't feel the weight of the world around you." Sounds like a promising promise, why does that promise sound so empty? A lie even.

"Yes! Plus you owe us! Haha, we came out here to have some fun! Learn how to live a little, because right now you are killing my vibe!" Zared said over the loud music.

"Yeah, Lina. It won't kill you." Ansa joined in on the conversation.

"Okay, fine." I am still so uncertain, but hey I don't want to be a downer. I made it all the way here after all, might as well get the full experience, what harm could it really do? I threw back the shot like it was the winning point. That thing stung going all the way down, some winning game shot. Maybe that is how a basketball player feels after they throw the game, that sting of regret, the burn of letting down not only their team, but their true young self before the pain and backstabbing. Before that 'I am only looking out for myself mentality.' Why did I feel like I was dying more than living?

"YES! Now you got it Lina!" Zared shouts, waving his hands from side to side. "Bottoms up ladies!" Continuing to give us shots after shots. After about six back to back shots I felt the room spinning, I needed to sit down. "Hey! Come here, follow me," he says, leading me to the dance floor. "Honey, you look extra sexy in this low cut silk black dress and lace black heels, we need to go show you off!" We make it to the dance floor and I can feel Zared dancing on me, pulling me closer. Ansa and Deni come and join in. We were dancing as if we were having sex with our clothes on.

All the grinding and touching was so much at once, that I finally broke free and searched for the nearest bathroom I could find. As I walk down the hallway searching, the walls seem to turn counterclockwise and the floor seems to be floating up at the same time. I struggle to catch my footing and stumble into a room. Thankfully there was a bathroom there. I made my way over and turned on the light, it was super bright. Why is a bathroom light that bright? I look into the mirror, and my reflection is blurry, it doesn't even look like me in this mirror. Who am I?

"If your goal was to turn me on tonight, you accomplished it." This strange yet familiar voice comes from behind me. I turn around and there he is, leaning in the doorway, with his head dropped looking at his glass, his shirt unbutton just enough to see his chest coming out as if his muscles were teasing me. The other hand is tucked into his front jean pocket while his veins are popping out of his arms taunting me of how his strength could hold me up in that doorway right now.

"I don't know what goal you are even talking about, plus why are you even at this frat party?"

"I was invited," he says looking up at me with such intensity as if he was ready to take this prey into his mouth.

"How were *you* invited?" I lean up against the bathroom sink ready to move away from him in a heartbeat.

"You ask a lot of questions you know."

"Call me intrigued."

"I am about to call you mine, did you know curiosity killed the cat. Let's just say, me, the one who brings you so much curiosity is about to kill that little kitty of yours."

"Uh," I say as I back up even further, knocking over things on the counter. "Oh no!" I turn around to start picking them back up and placing them back on the counter like it was before.

Then I feel his hands grab my waist and he leans into my ear, he begins to say, "I don't know why you are going to pick them back up they are just going to get knocked over again." While he says this I can't help but lean into him with my back-side. Those hands start caressing every inch of my body grabbing every right part proclaiming that it is all his. I moan at the moment he starts kissing that sweet spot on my neck. Why is this man so good at this? How does he know what to do with his hands so well? I take hold of the back of his neck, no longer fighting him just completely giving up control.

"Don't stop," I pleaded with him.

"Keep begging, I like it when you beg," his hand begins to pick up my dress and slowly taps every finger closer to my inner thigh, then up to my, "sweet paradise," he whispers.

"Cypher," I moan. Pushing myself forward because of the overwhelming feeling I was just experiencing that I now am leaning over the sink counter. I feel him grab my arm and turn me around, he kisses me on the lips then picks me up and places me on the counter. That very same mouth with nothing but pleasurable kisses starts racing with his hands going up to my inner thigh and his lips going down to it. I can feel his hands moving my panties to the side and his tongue speaks a whole new language. I wrap my legs around his neck, wanting him to keep talking. As I lean back grabbing his full head of hair I can't help but scream out, he suddenly gets up and smiles. I look at him, wondering what he has planned next in his head; he pulls me in closer and picks me up. We make our way into the bedroom and he throws me on the bed. As he is taking off his shirt I am examining every inch of his body and how much I want him inside of me. I sit up as he starts crawling over to me and he rips off my dress as if it was completely in the way and he didn't have the patience for either of us to take it off, we were past the point of waiting on each other. That was the first time I let him have me, all of me. The first time la petite mort, as the french would call it, was now going to be the ruling over my life.

Ugh, my head is pounding, why does everything seem like it is yelling in my face? I roll over and I see that I have my night shirt on; wait a minute, how did I even get back in my room? Did last night really happen or was everything just another crazy wet dream? As I move I feel pain in that area. Nope, last night really did happen. I get up, clumsily walking over to my bathroom and I run the shower. As I am removing my night shirt I notice marks all over my body. That man truly did claim me, didn't he; and with this pain he destroyed something all right. How many times did we do it last night? As I am in the shower I am taken back to any memory I had about last night. I remember him standing in the doorway, his kisses, and his touch. I throw on a shirt and shorts and head into the kitchen, but to my surprise Deni is already in the kitchen with a coffee in hand for me.

"Good morning, sunshine!"

"Good morning, please Deni no yelling." She hands me the coffee. "Oh, this is exactly what I needed. What happened last night? How did we get back home?"

"Well, we went searching for you last night, you disappeared for a long time and we saw you laying down on the bed sleep, half naked, which leads me to ask you a serious question, we weren't able to ask you last night because you were unconscious and we were worried, but do you remember any sexual activity that was non consensual?"

"Are you asking me if I remember if I was raped?"

"Yes! The way we found you was suspicious, if you were we need to go make this right!"

"Since when does going to the authorities really work out in this situation? The first question they will ask me is: Was I intoxicated? The moment I say yes, they won't take it seriously. Plus it would be news over campus because it happened at a frat party and I can already hear the name calling and the comments that 'I deserved it' and what not."

"Lina! For once stop thinking like that, this is serious, did you or did you not? I am really concerned here!"

"No, Deni I did not get raped."

"Okay! Good, do you know how you ended up half naked, with your dress ripped like an animal just attacked you? Are you even that strong to do that yourself?"

"Well..." I look away from her, taking another sip from my coffee, debating if

I should tell her the truth or make up a lie. The only reason why I would lie is because of how she has been acting, what if she really told Ansa about everything she pointed out yesterday with my mom, my dad, and even Cypher. Not only that I felt some shame of how everything happened, I wish I had been able to have had sex differently for the first time, not while I was drunk and with a man who is completely unapologetic and yet a complete package. On the other hand though, she is my best friend, I've never lied to her before and I have no actual proof that she told Ansa anything, so I respond with, "I ran into Cypher last night, and from what I remember we did it in that room you found me in." I look at her, waiting for her to respond to what I just admitted to.

"What! You and that sexy professor got it on last night, no way! Wow you go girl! Tell me every little dirty detail you remember, I have to know what a great screw he is." I laugh at her and start telling her the details I did remember. "No way!

Wow you must have been away longer than I thought. Well I guess for good reasons," she says while winking at me.

"Yeah," I give a light chuckle and take another sip of my coffee. "Hey, before you walk away, I had a question, just curious, but the other day I noticed something in your drawer when I was looking for Aspirin for you, how long have you been sexually active?"

"Haha, oh that, I was given that book from Ansa, and I recently became active. I never had the chance to tell you, with our schedules and all, but Zared and I have been sleeping around, nothing serious.

Look at us finally letting go and getting our cherries popped." As she begins to walk away, there is relief that my dream wasn't accurate at all. Deni wouldn't sleep with Cypher, would she?

Chapter FIVE

THE WEEKEND IS finally over and I am headed back to class, not hearing from Cypher all weekend made me worried. I felt as if I was just used by him; playing some sort of cat and mouse game. Since he finally caught me there is no longer a need for me. How dare he charm his way to getting inside of me and then turn around like it meant nothing to him. Is this what it feels like to be vulnerable with someone, the act of betrayal following behind? I stop at the cafe before class to get some breakfast and I see Dillon sitting with Rebecca, another classmate of ours. "Hey, Dillon."

"Oh, hey Paulina, or is it Lina now? You remember Rebecca right?"

"Yes, of course, hey Rebecca, and honestly either one, may I sit with you guys?"

"Yes, you may," Rebecca says in the sweetest voice.

"Have you guys finished the paper that is due this friday?"

"No, we haven't." Dillon is looking at Rebecca with such remorse. "I wouldn't give it much effort, Lina."

"Why do you say that Dillon? I thought you wanted to pass this class, that you needed to."

"Lina," Rebecca chimes in, "Writing your papers will not allow you to pass, nor any good grade that comes from it, this is not how you pass his class."

"What do you mean? How else would you pass this class?"

"Did you ever wonder why this class was given to you at the last possible moment before school even started? Or why is it around the corner at the end of the school completely far away from the nearest exit, not reaching any ray of sunlight?" I process what she is even asking me. "Lina, from where I sit watching you, you were already doomed to fail, the moment you first walked through the doors that day. There are still some of us who can still pass by the end of this year, and there are others who have exceeded their expiration and are trapped forever. Please help us figure out how to pass this class. This is my last chance and I want to get out of this life I am living because this class leads me into a dark hole that I can not get out of." Rebecca has a completely terrifying look on her face, as if she lost who she was and if she fails again then all hope is forever lost. "Watch out for his two little helpers, they have a way of accomplishing his goal."

"Who?" The moment I asked, Ansa and Zared both walked into the cafe. Dillon and Rebecca's eyes were overshadowed with fear.

"Watch out for those two, they are not who they seem to be. Most of the classmates are like us, wanting a way to get out before we are forever trapped walking this earth like zombies ." Before I could ask them more questions Ansa and Zared come walking right over to us. Dillon and Rebecca slump back into their chairs and grab their book bags leaving me at the table all by myself.

"Hey, Lina!" Ansa yells waving at me.

"Hey!" I say as I wave back.

"Just grabbing a quick bite to eat before class?" Zared asks observing me.

"Yeah, I didn't feel like just a protein bar. I knew it wasn't going to fulfill me this morning."

"No that won't. What do you say, we walk back to class together."

"Sure." We head back to the school and as I walk into class I notice Dillon and Rebecca looking at me with such concern. Before I could take a look around the classroom to examine everything they were pointing out to me earlier I heard his voice.

"Morning class, I know we have a lot to discuss before your paper is due. So quickly take your seats and let's get started," he says, glancing at me, paying me no attention as if I was a complete stranger to him. I couldn't help myself from being angry with him. I wanted to stand up and tell him off right here and right now, but I was afraid, what would everyone think of me? What would they say? Through all my animosity towards him I couldn't help but be drawn to him, the way his voice sounded in my ear, the way his kisses would move all around me. How he would give me that look, the look of how he couldn't wait one more minute to have me in his hands. As I am sitting here thinking of how I needed to have one more moment with him, to know that what happened between us was real, that I was still able to be useful, or even needed by such a magnificent man. I couldn't bear being one more second without him; taking him down, showing him how he could never forget me. "Okay, class that is all for today. I have a lot of work to catch up on, you may go and start working on your papers, you will need all the time in the world to please me," he says while sitting back down at his desk. As everyone walks by me leaving the room, I cannot help but stay still at my desk, lost in my thoughts conflicting between what I should do right now, I can tell him off, or I could go over there and ride him like a rodeo. "What are you still doing here Lina?" I jumped out of my seat and thought process, he was staring at me impatiently.

"Who do you think you are?" I say getting up from my desk marching over to him.

"Excuse me," he says, getting up from his desk walking over to me, grabbing my waist quicker than a cheetah, "I am the guy that makes you wet, the guy that you can't stop thinking about, the guy you want to overtake right here and right now." As he is telling me this he is pulling me in closer pulling my hair to bring my head back as he slowly nibbles on my neck. Oh, why can't I stay mad at this man, I have to let him know. I break free, he is shocked and confused. I get closer to him and start kissing him, taking off his belt and shirt pushing him to get on the desk. As he lays there on the desk I climb on him lifting up my dress saddling him then everything seems to fade in black...

"Lina!" Deni screams from her room.

"Yes, Deni."

"Do you know where my red dress is?"

"Yes, Deni I do; it's on me."

Deni comes bursting into my room, "What, why are you wearing it?"

"Well, I saw it and wanted to wear it, so I took it."

"You just took it without asking me?"

"Yeah, isn't that what you always do, take without permission," I say, turning away from the mirror looking at her carelessly.

"Plus she looks smoking hot in this dress," Zared says, rushing in with a couple of drinks. "This girl knows how to have fun after her first party we took her to a couple months ago! You have changed and I am liking it, definitely turning me on right now!" I give a flirtatious laugh, winking then taking a sip out of my glass.

"Really Zared, you are just going to say that in front of me? Lina you are really going to flirt back?" I roll my eyes and turn away.

"Oh, stop babe it was just a joke plus you know you have done worse to..."

"Shut up Zared!"

"Look," I interrupted their conversation. "I don't have time for any of your guys' drama. I will be at Nick's party if you want to join."

"You know we will be there," Ansa says, coming into the bedroom.

"Fine, no drama please or else I won't hesitate to kick you guys out." I head into the chair in the corner of the room to start putting on my heels. Deni follows behind after all her rage and starts yelling.

"Who do you think you are!" Deni yells at me still in her emotional rampage. "Just because you screwed the professor and now he doesn't want anything to do with you, you started to become this egotistical witch who thinks she is better than everyone taking your anger out on others!"

I get up from out of my chair completely unfazed and walk towards Deni, and whisper in her ear, "I am still screwing him." I bump into her and walk away.

"Deni, maybe you should stay home and pamper yourself," Zared tells her.

"What!"

"That is what is best, Deni, for you to be alone tonight," Ansa buds in. We all walk out of the apartment leaving Deni behind, not taking a second moment to look back as the door closes.

"Lina!" Nick yells out to me. "Babe come over here and join us in playing beer pong!"

"Okay, but I want to play it with a twist, for every time any of us makes it in, the other player not only drinks but also removes a part of their clothing, Nick go ahead and play opposite of me."

"Oooo, I love a woman who can take charge and come up with great ideas."

"Yeah, I bet you do, Zared come be my partner; Ansa, go and team up with Nick."

"You got it girl!" Zared rushes over to my side.

The end was near, down to the last cup on both sides and it was my turn to shoot, come on Lina, you got this you can score. As I flick my wrist the ball is circling the cup, a slow motion moment like in a movie, and it goes in. "In your face! Haha, time to take it off."

"I will take it off alright," he grabs my hand leading me to the back of the house, "first we need to go for a swim!" We jump into the pool. I swim off to an abandoned corner, with Nick swimming close behind. As he quickly catches up to me he grabs me and places me on top of him, "Girl, I don't know who you are but you are definitely something else," he starts kissing me everywhere, "so freakishly refreshing."

The thing is I didn't know who I was anymore. Ever since Cypher made it clear that he was just using me, I became numb. Drinking every night, smoking weed in between, and having sex with other guys. Yes, I still am screwing Cypher, if I can't have him in a relationship, well this is as good as anything else, at least I can still have him some way, I am able to still and always be needed by him. After all he was the man who led me to this unfulfilling rabbit hole. As I finish being with Nick, I get up out of the pool and head to the outhouse. As I try to compose myself I start feeling like complete crap, I literally use these guys for my self pleasure as if I have some worth to prove, like I have to gain some sort of power or even some sense of control. Denying my brokenness I truly have inside. Yet none of this truly satisfies me at all. I feel like I am constantly fighting, the scary part is I don't even know who or what I am fighting against. Even though I am with Nick I can't help but think about Cypher and how he makes me feel. As I sit back in the chair, the lights go dark and I suddenly get tied up. "Help! Someone help me!"

"No one can hear you honey," a strange voice in the distance calls out.

"Scream all you want, no one wants to listen to you," another voice says getting closer.

"Well, well, well if it isn't one of my most prized possessions all tied up, just how I like it," Cypher comes closer to my face with a grin.

"What are you doing? What kind of game is this? Let me go now!" I demanded. I hear nothing but voices all around me.

"No, see I can't do that. When you made a connection with me I became a part of you, you will forever be mine there is no freedom for you when this year is done." All these hands came around me possessing every inch of my body, pulling me down. I couldn't breathe.

"No! Let me go! I didn't ask for this!"

"Forever you will be unsatisfied and tortured. Souviens-toi de la petite mort? You died with me and now you will live with this darkness all around you, you are my prodigy, my puppet," all the hands that used to be around me became chains in his hands. Then he began to laugh maliciously as if he won and no one could ever defeat him.

"Died?!"

Chapter SIX

"LINA! LET'S GO. I am not going to miss my flight to go back home just because you can't find your phone charger. We will get you another one," Deni says to me.

"Okay I am coming, I'll just buy another one," I say annoyed. "Just go wait for me in the car," I demanded. I hear her huff and slam the door. Ever since Deni and I had our lashing out moment it really hasn't calmed down from there. It seems that we have had many arguments lately, our friendship no longer solid, slowly breaking with every word we speak to each other and don't.

It is officially winter break and two weeks since that horrible dream at that party. I am actually excited to get out of here for three and half weeks. I needed to get away from Cypher. I would see him regularly, more than most people really knew, he would always know about my hook ups with other guys and be completely turned on, he liked being the other guy. It almost seemed that he liked that more guys were falling into my seduction. The way he would attack me after class was his own way of saying I was his queen, he promised me power. I was no longer that shy little girl from Cortez, Colorado. I was a woman who got everything she wanted when she wanted it. If it was there for the taking I took it, unapologetically.

There was still a part of me that cared for the way I treated everyone, I burned some bridges here in just a few months. People knowing what they knew still came around as if they were trying to see if they would be the one to break my barrier and expose who I am. How could they do that when my identity was far lost. Many people feared me, many people admired me, yet in the end they all just truly hated me. Was there anyone in my life who really loved me?

I barely got through this semester. My priorities have gotten all mixed up lately. I am glad that I still succeeded in my classes. I don't know how I would have let my mother know how I had failed my first semester. At Least with Professor Cypher's class he said that he only believes in the one final grade at the end of the year. Surprisingly though when I looked online for my grades his class was not listed. No class, no grade, no GPA affected. I wasn't too concerned, should I have been I wouldn't be where I am now.

I am definitely not looking forward to going home. If you aren't aware by now my mother and I are more like acquaintances than anything else. In other words if she could have it her way we are associated with each other through a mutual friend. Since I have been here for four months I've only talked to her twice. Quick 5 minute conversations if you even want to call them that.

My dad was my best friend. Unfortunately he died when I was 6 years old due to a robbery gone bad. Wrong place at the wrong time kind of thing. He is my hero. I like to think he died due to carrying out a special mission and he risked his life in order to save others. Ever since his passing my mother shut off the world, well mainly me. In and out of clubs and bars. Coming home with different men every night. I couldn't help but think that maybe she was either looking for my dad in one of these men or that she knew that was something impossible to obtain again so she cut her loss and was filled with complete hopelessness.

As I put on my coat I notice a shadow standing outside my door. I swing the door open and what do I know it's Cypher.

"Well hello darling," he says with a smirk not slightly moving an inch.

"Why are you here?"

"Oh come on, you are not going to give me a kiss goodbye?"

"For what? Now please move out of my way. I have a flight to catch."

"Headed back home to see mommy, huh? I hope she welcomes you with open arms, if she doesn't you know whose arms you can be lifted in. I'll only be an hour away from you, I will be at a bachelor party in that area. I've already sent you the address to the club and the place I'll be staying at. You should really stop relying on trying to receive the love of others, when all you need is me."

I push past him trying not to listen to anything he just said and yet it is sticking stronger than glue in my head. "Love, ha do you even know what that is?"

"Do you?" chuckling through his teeth, watching me walk away.

Feeling defeated. Ashamed even, I have fantasized of what love could be, should be. Being in this web with Cypher has made me question it all, even its existence.

I got into the car with Deni, but before we could drive away Ansa and Zared came running to us.

"Hey you crazy kids! We just wanted to wish you guys a safe trip," Ansa says.

"Yes, and babe let me know when you landed so I can phone sex you later," Zared says with a grin and gives Deni a kiss. To be surprisingly honest I am shocked to see this thing still going. I never saw Deni settling with anyone, especially not during her college years. She has always been so free spirited and ever since she has been with Zared she looks more and more drained, definitely not the Deni I knew.

I am staring out the passenger window trying to escape this reality, the world that has been created around me. Hoping and wishing I could leave to escape to somewhere else. No more Colorado, no more Georgetown, and definitely no more Cypher. I couldn't help but notice Dillon and Rebecca. They are staring at me telling me to look at my phone by pointing to their phones. I pull out my phone and it reads:

Dillon: Don't fall for any more of his tricks, no matter how much he strives to push you to go see him run away.

Rebecca: If I were you I wouldn't come back here. Or you won't be recognizable to the point where not even the cops could identify your body.

As I am reading this I felt a shiver of fear crawling down my spine. What was this warning about? What did they know that I didn't? I looked up so fast to see them, but Deni was driving out of the parking lot like some professional race car driver. As I started to text back, my phone died. Go figure, the irony of trying to find out the truth to what is really going on leads to something always dying, or even someone.

As I am headed on to the plane, I feel a turning in my stomach. I am not sure if it was those scary messages, my lack of eating this morning, or the fact that I have to see my mother. As I am sitting in my chair waiting for lift off Deni is passing me some shooters from the snack cart she just smuggled.

"Here, take this and this" she hands me a pill. "It will help you relax, you don't look too good."

"What is this? And you know you shouldn't steal this, put it back."

"Oh, you can be all tough around campus, Queen Lina, everyone falling to your knees, but you don't want to have a hint of liquor on your breath because you're worried about what your mommy thinks. Face it you are still that little shy girl, you are such a poser."

"Shut up!" I snapped at her, "Who are you really looking out for? Oh I am sorry if you are jealous that it is me everyone is looking at and no one wants to look your way, the only reason you are even a bit noticed is because you are socially acquainted with me. Go wash away your envy before your parents disown you for not being the most powerful woman on campus."

"Here, take it and just pass out, I'll wake you when we land," Deni says, completely shattered and broken. She and I both knew that the only reason she hasn't pushed me away is because of the attention she has gotten with me around and if it came down to Ansa and Zared having to choose, they would drop her in the next heartbeat, as if their last heartbeat depended on it.

"Fine, give it to me" I take the pill and the shooter and I down it. I put my head back, closing my eyes, feeling the sting of the liquor slowly going down and next thing I knew the sting became numbing and everything seemed to fade and move in slow motion. I drift off into a different space, a different world, I have finally escaped my reality.

"Wake up, Lina. Come on we are here" Deni is shaking me awake.

"Huh? Already? Okay I am coming." I slowly start moving in my seat trying to get my seatbelt off so I can get up. "Wait

Deni my seatbelt is stuck I can't get out, come and help me please."

She comes back to me smiling, "Oh now you want some help, looks like no one's here to help you."

"Deni, what are you talking about, help me please."

I look at her completely confused, she is supposed to be my best friend. How could she not help me? Before I can say something I hear a voice in the distance.

"Hello babe."

"Zared!? Please help me get out of here"

"No can do, I'm under strict orders not to."

"From who?"

"Me"

"Cypher? Why are you here?"

"I am always here, I want you right there because I want you to watch." Cypher starts to kiss Deni and she begins to moan. I get furious because I am the only one who should make that sound for him. I try to look away and Zared

comes to me grabbing my face to force
me to watch. As I continue to watch I see
Cypher removing her panties and dropping them to the ground. Continuing to
kiss her he runs his hands in between her
and she can't control herself. "Say it Lina,
I need to hear you say it," he says, staring
at me the entire time. A part of me knew
what he was telling me to say to him, I
just knew that if I did, something terrible
was going to happen. As he is removing
his fingers from her he brings them to his
lips and licks them, she and Zared laugh.
Cypher walks over to me and says, "If you
say it, I'll let you go and you can come
join in on the fun." He brushes those
same fingers across my lips and begins
to kiss me.

"No!" I scream at him, "I will not!" The
look on his face grew dark and cold,
worse than I have ever seen before and
he reached after me. "No!"

"Lina! Wake up! Lina stop hitting me,
wake up!" Deni is persistent in trying to
wake me up.

"What! Oh thank you, it was just a dream," I say breathing heavily. Sweat is dripping down my forehead.

"Ma'am are you okay?" the steward came over to ask. As I looked at her I couldn't help but notice the other passengers around her, all giving me a look as if they knew, they knew who I am and what I've done, what I dreamt about, I felt complete shame.

"Yes, I am fine thank you, just a bad dream. May I have some water please."

"Certainly, let me go get that for you." As she walks away Deni has a concerned look on her face.

"Deni please don't ask, I don't want to talk about it."

"Okay, I won't" she slouches back into her chair. "You know though if you ever want to change your major from battling the mind, you can become a boxer and knock some people down physically. Start calling you Lina Ali, those punches sting like a bee." We both look at each other and start laughing.

"Oh my, when was the last time we laughed like this."

"Probably when you decided that skinny dipping in the Potomac River was a great idea."

"Ha, well how was I to know that sharks live there, good thing he wasn't in a mood for stopping for a snack on the way home."

"Here you are ma'am" the steward hands me some water.

"Thank you"

"Yeah who knew that you would be the one to persuade us to do that."

"If I remember correctly I just came up with the part of swimming in the river the skinny dipping part was all you. And the way you presented your argument I can say you haven't lost your touch." I give Deni a light shove and both of us are smiling.

"I guess you are right, this is a gift I am not ashamed to have. Look I am sorry for how I've been lately, college isn't as glamorous as everyone made it seem to be. I know that doesn't give me any excuse to treat you that way. Can you forgive me?"

"Already long gone, plus I am at fault too, please forgive me for the awful things I have said to you. Just because they are things I wanted to say to you at the moment doesn't make it right for me to say such hurtful things out of spite. I should be expressing my words out of love." How could I speak out of love when I knew no love.

"Water under the bridge, hey look we are here. Home sweet home!"

Great! Landed at CEZ, why did the 4 hours have to go by so fast?

As we get off the plane there is a tall man in a suit and tie holding up a sign:

Paulina Saville

"Dang Lina, your mom is definitely getting the younger ones, he is so fine! Can't keep her waiting."

"Yeah, I guess not." As I walk up I can't help but examine him. Tall and built, not excessively but you can tell he hits the gym at least three times a week. Eyes are hazel, filled with such kindness and hope. Dirty blonde hair so perfectly cut and styled and his beard is nicely shaved. "I am Paulina Saville."

"Well hello Ms. Saville, my name is Ethan Arlo, I am here to drive you home," he smiles at me, of course this man has some perfect teeth, why wouldn't he? It's not like being on the front cover of a magazine is enough, nope he has to take the billboards too. "Please let me take your bags and follow me."

"Bags follow, me take."

"Excuse me?"

"She means thank you, please lead the way." Deni jumps in to save the day as I am paralyzed to even speak or move because of what just came out of my mouth. How come all my confidence ran away from me, I haven't acted like this since the first day I met Cypher. Who is this guy? He just came out of nowhere. Deni is pushing me to walk so I don't lose him in the crowd.

"Here you are Ms. Saville, and I am sorry I didn't catch your name."

"Deni, Deni Jackson"

"Well Ms. Jackson, a pleasure to meet you," he says, shaking her hand and then opening up the car door for us. Our bags get put into the trunk.

"Girl, what a gentleman! I want him."

"Too bad Deni, I'm sure he is taken by my mother." The moment I say those words he comes into the car. "Hey, Ethan, can you stop at J's? We could really go for a bite to eat."

"Sorry Ms. Saville I am ordered to take you straight home, I am told both of your parents have put together a dinner party for your arrival."

"Great." I sigh and slouch in my seat. As we were starting to drive away I was hoping we would hit traffic, hit every red light even, just as long as we didn't get to the most jeweled house in all of Cortez. I looked up and I couldn't help but look at Ethan through the mirror, how could someone like him make me so fluster?

Have I lost my touch, was my reputation already going downhill? Will this be the man to try and knock my walls down? He must have felt my eyes on him because he looks up right at me and gives me a simple smile and looks back on the road. Wait a minute isn't that what I am supposed to do, play hard to get. Oh no if this is a game you want to play then okay, I will play. I smirk and push back my hair, reaching for my sunglasses and put them on. I end up looking out the window, not giving him another glance.

We pull up into the driveway, dang! Look who is outside waiting for us to get out, waiting to welcome their guests of honor. My mother is always looking to put on a world class performance so she can get her high. She lives for that standing ovation. Mr. and Mrs. Jackson looked extremely excited and happy waving at us. Ethan parks the car and turns it off, quickly getting out to open the door.

"Mom! Dad!" Deni jumps out of the car practically sprinting to her parents with open arms.

"Oh my sweet angel cake! How was the flight? Not too bad I hope?" Mrs. Jackson wraps her arms around Deni welcoming her with a warm embrace.

"Not at all, I missed you guys so much"

"We missed you too, come inside it is a bit cold, come on," the three of them go inside.

"Well, are you happy to see me, Paulina?" My mother standing at the top of the stairs glaring down at me, waiting for her well *deserved* response.

"Hello, mom, I guess I can ask the same thing." As I say walking towards her.

"Look, let's have a peaceful few weeks, I have some very important business partners coming in and out of here and I don't need you or your attitude to ruin it for me. So stay out of my way and we will be okay. In the meantime during all events that you will be attending, we will fake it and put on a loving show."

"I wouldn't want to ruin your precious reputation, mother."

"Looks like you've already broken this image of being my precious daughter with that alcohol on your breath."

"No mother you have broken that image about me a long time ago, I am just now tired of trying to constantly restore that perfect image."

Chapter SEVEN

"SHE SAID THAT to you?"

"Are you really surprised at this point Deni?"

"I guess not, I just can't believe that this is where your relationship lies."

"Trust me if she wasn't worried about what everyone thinks of her she would have gotten rid of me a long time ago."

"How do I look?" Deni comes out posing like a supermodel. Getting ready for another Mrs. Saville dinner party.

"Deni, you look absolutely stunning!"

"Thank you, hey do you remember when we would play dress up with your moms makeup and jewelry?"

"Yes! She was so mad at us because we lost that ruby ring. I wonder where we hid it, we had to stash it away so the imaginary cops didn't get us."

"We were definitely pros at being jewelry thieves."

"We were the perfect partners in crime," pausing for a minute trying to remember back on a memory, "now that I think of it, that was probably not the best game to play at that time; given what happened and all," I let out a deep sigh.

"Oh wow, you are right. I am so sorry Lina. We didn't really know back then, you can't blame yourself for how your mom reacted." Deni comes close to me, holding my hand. "Here let me help you with your hair." As she is putting my hair up I couldn't help remember the way my mom did react when she noticed her ruby ring missing. She came bursting into my room, yelling at me telling me how I am such an evil child for taking her most precious ring and to even play such a vile game. She threw her empty glass at me, thankfully Deni was there to push me out of the way so the glass could hit the wall behind me. She told me as long as that ring was gone, so was her daughter. After she stormed out, Deni and I cleaned up the glass and spent hours trying to remember where we placed that ring. I cried many nights in my room feeling all alone. I am so thankful I had Deni with me during that time, though I was disowned from my own mother it felt like I still had a sister. "There, you look absolutely gorgeous. Now we have to be on our best behavior for the well-prestigious parents down there."

"Ha, yeah let's make a deal to cause trouble when we leave this dinner party, you know it is more for them and it will last for hours." We just laugh as we are mocking our parents. Then there is a knock on the door. "Come in."

"Excuse me Ms. Saville and Ms. Jackson, your parents are awaiting your presence."

"Thank you Ethan let them know we are on our way."

"Will do ma'am."

"Ethan?" I catch him before he closes the door behind him.

"Yes, Ms. Saville"

"You are free to call me Paulina and her Deni."

"Yes ma'am," as he starts to shut the door he stops and looks at me with those bold eyes. "I was only waiting on your permission." He smiles so graciously, practically melting me where I stand. His very words pierce into my ever being of a woman who deserves to be respected. I simply smile back and he shuts the door. The moment the door closed it was like a time bomb went off in my cheeks, I couldn't help but glow, grinning from ear to ear.

"Girl, he might be into you. Wouldn't he make a fine treasure to your collection, and a great way to stick it to your mother that you are sleeping with her man."

"No, I wouldn't go there, plus he seems different, I will leave him be."

"What!? I really hope you reconsider."

"Come on, we need to head down stairs before one of them starts running rampant."

We head down stairs and are laughing uncontrollably remembering all the times we had in this house. The memories that I hold are precious to my heart, such happiness it brought and then my mother begins to speak, "Well look at the lovely women gracing us with their presence." Now I can't help but remember how cold hearted this place was for me; nothing but trauma, anger, and sadness filled up inside of me.

"So Paulina your mother here tells me you are doing quite well for yourself at Georgetown. How was your first semester?" Mr. Carter says while approaching me.

"Oh, it had its challenging moments and..."

"She is being modest, she has told me how everyone wants to be part of her study group because she understands and grasps the content so well, why everyone else is constantly struggling," my mother interrupts, mainly to praise herself for raising such an achieving daughter. Little did she know I lied to her.

People wanted to be around me because I was a great party host. And passing this semester with a 3.5 GPA. Yes that is barely passing to me, because that is exactly how my mother would tell it. Telling me how I am such a failure and I am not living up to my potential so therefore I am a disappointment.

"Wow! That is extremely amazing Paulina. Please there is no need to be so modest here, own it. You are an outstanding student, don't downsize yourself to fit in." Mr. Carter sounds so confident and proud, knowing who he is. It also seemed he was so proud of me for the woman I am becoming, too bad he is proud of a lie.

My mother takes Mr. Carter away showing him her new painting that she recently bought that was such a trea- sured piece to her heart. As they walk off Mrs. Carter approaches me, "What he says is true, just always remember though there is a fine line between arrogance and confidence. It is right to walk in the inheritance that is yours to help benefit something or someone far greater than you, the moment you start glorifying yourself is when it becomes a problem. Don't lose yourself by trying to find yourself." She says all this staring me deep in my soul. Before I could ask her what she was talking about or even give her a thank you, my brain was all scrambled trying to understand what just happened. She had already walked away to catch up with Mr. Carter. How can simple words pierce through me and break down a solid foundation? At least I thought it was solid.

"Lina!

"Deni!" I say as she comes running to me in her heels, taking hold of my arms. Giving me such a crazy look.

"When can we leave, I want to go to a party, go to a park, go hiking even."

'Hiking? You don't like to hike. Matter of fact you despise it," I say trying to break free from her grip. When did she get so strong?

"I'll take it up now, if it gets me out of here," she starts to pace back and forth. "How many times can you answer the same question? It's like going to the doctor's office, just look at my chart. I guess in this case just jump in the conversation, I see you listening to me anyways, you already know the answer, better yet why..."

"Girl, breathe. I get it, I do. Let's stick it out for tonight. You were so eager to come back home, let's at least be the children that our parents are presenting us to be this evening. Okay?"

"Fine."

"Deni, can you please come here dear, Mrs. Whitler has a gift for you."

"Okay mother I'll be right there." She smiles waving to her mother. She turns to me looking frantic, "You owe me big, you know she gives gifts that she knitted with her cats shedding. I can't believe you made me stay."

"Don't want to keep Mr. Nibbles waiting," I say laughing, waving to her goodbye. Seeing her off to fight her own battle of doom. "You got this soldier!" She turns around giving me an angry look with a fist.

As I stood in this room I could see how truly empty it was, I had to remove myself and get my coat to head outside. I needed to breathe. Being in freezing weather was a lot better option than being in that house. As I stood outside, I couldn't help but notice the cold air escaping my lips. Really thinking about how this is similarly created the same way fog is created. How crazy that fog allows us to not see what is right before us. Causing us to stand between what is seen and unseen. I was remembering a time when I read into weather and symbolism, that some find fog to lead us into isolation or even death. What is once so natural becomes unnatural. We can see life here all around us, when it comes to death we don't see it coming and going.

We know that it is inevitable, yet there are many speculations of what happens when we die. My question is more of do we see death in the land of the living? Makes you think if Hollywood producers see something we don't; we have many movies and shows about zombies, the dead among the living. The dead chasing down every living being one by one, either as a meal or to make them turn into one of them. It goes for vampires. At least they are hidden in plain sight. Perhaps that's what makes them the most terrifying, mostly known. How they lure their victims with charm, deception, and manipulation. Leaving their prey vulnerable, unable to have a guard and fight back...

"Hello, Ms. Paulina"

I hear a voice in the distance breaking my concentration. I start to look out trying to see who it was. What do you know, "Hello, Ethan."

"What are you doing out here in the cold?"

"I just needed to get out of there, it got a bit too stuffy for my taste. Why are you out here?"

"Well to be completely honest I was sent to look for you."

"Of course you were."

"Well if it helps, I knew you were out here, so I decided to look here last to give you a bit of some breathing room, I could tell from the moment I saw you at the airport that you did not want to be here, but didn't want to be at your school either."

Who is this man, how does he see me? Why does he see me? He doesn't know me and yet I feel like he knows me better than I know myself. "What angle is he trying to get at?"

"Who is he?"

In complete shock that my inner thought just came out in front of him, made me fall into complete embarrassment, I had two options: either get away from his question or answer it. "He is you," I say, trying to be confident that my outburst was what I intended.

"Well, I have no angle, no goal, or agenda in the aspect of hurting you or even getting you to break down your wall. I could say that I knock on the door of your heart in hopes that you would be willing to let me in. I want to mend what is broken inside, helping you to see and know that love is more than a feeling, an everyday choice, an umbrella of all that is good."

I am absolutely surprised. My eyes widened, hands sweating, heart racing, and legs shaking mainly because I was legit freezing my butt off, not the point, at the fact that this man just said what he said. He can tell I was stunned and I believe that was an understatement of what just happened here. He couldn't help but smile, looking at me and looking away. His smile was different, not in a malicious way like I got you in my hook, it was genuine that if I didn't say anything at all that was the greatest compliment he could ever get from me and he was more than thankful to receive it. As he

103

was looking into me saying these words I couldn't help but feel that he was looking past everything I had ever done, it's like he knew. Everything being presented to him on a silver platter that he could have just eaten and disposed of, instead he took that silver platter and washed it, not caring of what has been done, what is being done, or whatever will be done. Who can see someone with such compassion? Who can receive such great ammo to use against your enemy, intended for their demise and yet still cease? "I think I need to head back inside now."

"Okay, well let me give you this, it's my phone number. I must leave for the night. When you are ready to be willing, I'll be waiting. Doesn't matter how long it takes, you are worth it."

I grab the number and walk away going back inside. Me being behind a wooden door didn't seem to be doing its job correctly in keeping people out. Because I could still feel his warm presence right beside me.

Chapter EIGHT

"PAULINA, " MY mother's knocking enters into my dreams, pounding in my head like a migraine. I can hear her burst into my room, because the 2 seconds of waiting was far too long. "Paulina, wake up, we will be late."

As I turn over the covers and look at her as to why she has to have everything on a schedule. "Did you know patience is a virtue, mother."

"I had my patience in carrying you, and look at where that got me. Now get up we have to get you fitted, and we are having lunch with the Jones'. Just because school says you have a break doesn't mean that is how the real world works. So get up and let's go. I'll give you 15 minutes."

"Or what you will send your bouncer to come get me?" As I say rolling out of the bed.

"I just might," she says with a smug on her face while walking out of my room and closing the door.

"Whatever." I head to my closet trying to find something decent to wear for our lunch meeting that I have to attend. After everything last night I couldn't help but think of what Ethan told me, and how I am going to run into him again, maybe I should look really special today. For the first time, in a long time I was genuinely excited to see someone else. So with the 15 minutes that I had...

"12 more minutes Paulina."

"Okay! I didn't think I ordered a timer for my stay these next few weeks." Well 12 minutes now, I was going to put some extra care into how I looked. Curling my hair, wearing some light make-up and throwing on some jewelry.

I head down stairs and you can see the look on my mothers face was full of rage. "Do you think it took you long enough, and for what?"

"What do you mean I'm sure I beat your stupid timer you said I had 30 seconds."

"Yeah you see this, you came down in 32 seconds." She shows me on her phone. Speaking of phones, I still needed to get a charger.

"I am sorry mother, I will be more prompt next time." She gives me that look that says not to start with her. We head out and there is Ethan smiling, waiting for us.

"Good morning, Mrs. Saville," he opens the door for my mother first.

"Good morning handsome, don't you seem very radiant this morning. I can't help but to think it is because of my dashing good looks."

"You have a very beautiful smile Mrs. Saville, you should use it more."

"You are far too kind dear," he shuts the car door because she is *a lady,* and ladies don't ever scooch according to her.

I walk around to the other side and as I walk over with him he says nothing. I felt a bit broken, why is he not saying anything to me? "Here you are Ms. Paulina."

"Yeah, thanks." I grab the handle and shut the door on him.

"Paulina, what is the matter with you? Why are you being so rude to Ethan? Please don't tell me this is how you are when you get jealous, if so stop wearing it, it does not look good on you, it really brings out the wrinkles in your forehead."

Before I could say anything Ethan got into the car and started driving off. I didn't know what it was, but I couldn't tell my mother off. If so, what would I really say? Would it hurt me more to throw darts at her or let it go? I was not sure, so I sat there quietly until we reached the boutique.

"We are here darling, come on," Ethan quickly gets out of the car to open up the door for my mother. "Ethan please go enjoy yourself in the cafe that they have here, we might be here awhile."

"Yes ma'am I certainly will, thank you."

"Angela!" my mother yells out chasing her down.

"Eva! Come in, I want to show you what I've made special for you and your daughter."

They both walked into the boutique forgetting that I was even there, oh well. Ethan finally had let me out of the car and I looked right past him as if he was no one to me. Walking away from him until...

"Hey, Paulina," Ethan grabs my hand to turn me around to face him. "What is wrong, you seemed very angry in the car?"

"I'm glad you noticed something about me."

"What does that mean?"

"Hello, you complimented my mother on how she looked and I am over here trying to look a bit more present-able for you."

"Why?"

"Really, why? I'm sorry did last night not happen or was I still hallucinating from earlier. Did you not just tell me how you felt?"

"Yes, last night was real. What I meant was why would you get all dolled up for me? I don't like you based on your outer appearance, yes I do find you attractive being knitted wonderfully and fearfully, a gift from above, that I am honored to be presented with. I have an affection towards you based on who you are, what is inside of you. I complimented your mother on her smile because she does have a wonderful smile especially when it is genuine, for someone who is just as broken and the fact that she can still find a genuine smile to give is a beautiful thing. I didn't compliment her on her outfit or flashy jewelry because none of that matters to me. What is it that someone gains the world, all its treasures and still loses themselves, their soul. I am sorry if that hurt you, it was not my intention. I only intend for you to understand that I find you beautiful, that only someone with eyes that can see, can notice your beauty reflects from the inside out."

"How could you know who I am? And on the inside I am just a horrible person you don't know the things I've done, or said."

"There you are Paulina. Your mother is inside trying on her dress and you need to get yours fitted." Angela wraps her arms around me, not paying any attention to Ethan. Guiding me right passed him. As I looked at him he was sad, his eyes showed the sorrow of my words. Saying to me that I am much more than what has already been done and he wants to open my eyes to a different perspective, something much larger than what I've been trapped in.

"Ta-da!" My mother comes out of the fitting room, "This is extraordinary! You have really outdone yourself here Angela."

"Thank you Eva, go on Paulina, head inside there and let's see what alterations we need to make."

"Yes ma'am."

"Ma'am? I've never heard you say that before."

"I guess I am trying something new." I head into the dressing room, trying on this incredible dress. I couldn't help but think of what Ethan had said to me. Was it still wrong for me wanting to get a compliment, maybe something that meant deeper than, "that dress makes you look beautiful," or "wow you look amazing." Was it wrong that I wanted the kind of compliment that he had mentioned?

"Paulina dear, don't keep us waiting."

"Coming Angela," as I come out they both just gasp. Angela is in complete awe that her artwork has come to life. She had created this day and night, designed especially for me and the time was here for her endless hours of fabrication for this exact moment; no longer a creation stuck in her head or words just spoken, a hand crafted project carrying out what it was meant to do. Tears streamed down her rosy cheeks.

"Wow, you look perfect! Let me go get my pins and needles, I'll be right back."

"Yes, that dress is perfect," my mother said with such jealousy as she sipped on her champagne.

"Thanks."

Angela walks in with such a smile on her face, so big and joyful that if there was a smiling contest, she would have won the contest 5 years in a row. She takes her pins and needles and starts adjusting some areas of the dress.

"Let's not gain any weight until the evening you are to wear this dress, Paulina."

"When will this evening be, mother?"

"Christmas Eve will be the party of the century, that is what our lunch meeting will be about. I am trying to land a deal with the Jones'."

"Well I guess I need to cancel my all you can eat buffet that I ordered to attend your house later on this evening."

"All done!" Angela says so nothing more will arise from our conversation.

"Thank you Angela," I say heading back to the fitting room, taking off the dress.

We leave the boutique, now heading to see the Jones'. I wished this day would be over with. All these fake smiles and pleasantries were giving me a headache. How much longer do I have to keep faking this? How long have I been faking to be happy? As I was trying to remember the last time I was truly happy, I was leading myself into a darker hole of depression. Could I ever really be happy? As we entered the parking lot of our next destination, I couldn't help but make a deep sigh, getting ready to put on a show yet again. Lights, camera, action, I should get paid at this point. My mother and I get out of the car and without hesitation my mother starts to yell, "Patricia, Eric, how wonderful for you guys to invite us to lunch!"

"Of course Eva, this lunch date was long overdue." Mrs. Jones says with such eloquence.

"I would agree," Mr. Jones approaches in his business casual outfit with his hands in his pocket. He smiles with such charm. "Plus we needed to see how Paulina was holding up at Georgetown, I am sorry that we couldn't make it last night to your welcome home party."

"It is okay Mr. Jones, you didn't miss much. Plus the way you guys help us out, the least we could do is give you guys your own V.I.P access." I say so pleasingly to the ear that I can see Mr. Jones' eyebrow raise up, intrigued. Looking at me in a seductive way.

"Excuse me sir, your table is ready."

"Thank you Colton," Mr. and Mrs. Jones walked ahead of us with our host and my mother turned to me.

"What was that all about?"

"What? I just let them know how their generosity all these years hasn't gone unnoticed and we appreciate them enough to take the time to thank them properly and more intimately."

"Sure it was, please don't use your sarcasm for this meal, let all your smart alec comments go out the window today, can you do that for me?"

"Fine." In a way I was glad that no one noticed how I was trying to seduce Mr. Jones. I couldn't help it, the way he stood there looking at me with those deep blue eyes, not looking like an age over 30, with his built body. Having that salt and pepper thing going on. The way he walked in like he owned the place, honestly I wouldn't be surprised if he owned it.

"How do you like the restaurant? I bought it and refurbished it, it was a complete dump when I found it, but saw a lot of potential."

Well there that goes.

"It is magnificent Eric, the chandelier really makes this place classy."

"Thank you Eva, how about you Paulina?"

"Oh, uh, the menu looks pretty cool with how everything you sell here fits on one page and all."

Mr. Jones starts to laugh, then Mrs. Jones follows in. My mother, really concerned, still managed to let out a laugh. "You are quite the comedian, I needed a good laugh. Well if you have any suggestions on what I could add to the menu please let me know sometime and we can take a look."

"Thank you Mr. Jones."

"So Eric, how are the festive arrangements coming along for your upcoming Christmas party?"

"Only you Eva can get straight to the point, I find it very admirable," Mrs. Jones says.

"I believe there are times to cease the opportunity, and there are times to dangle the bait a little bit, just enough to get a taste," Mr. Jones said to the group, but when they were not looking he stared at me drinking his whisky. "But since we are here and I would like us to eat as friends and not make this a business lunch, I have thought about your proposal Eva..."

"We would love for you to be our party planner, we have seen how you truly have a gift. We wanted to let you know now, given that Christmas Eve is in a week to see how well you can work under pressure. We want to push you further into your potential. Now there will be exclusive people at this party and if they like your work you will come highly recommended," Mrs. Jones screams, practically jumping out of her seat. I couldn't help but notice how excited she was for my mother. I thought that was quite sweet to see someone, a close friend, genuinely happy for someone they cared about.

"Yes, and they are the type to plan events with short notices, so think of this as a training ground," Mr. Jones buds in to put in his unbiased advice.

"Thank you so much! You guys really know how to keep a woman waiting."

"We will meet tomorrow to go over the arrangements, but today let's enjoy the company of one another."

"You got it Eric, no more work talk from me."

David the waiter comes over to us and asks, "Is the table ready to order?"

"Yes David, Mrs. Jones and I will have our usual, and whatever their heart desires."

"Yes David, may I please have the Cordon Bleu"

"Yes ma'am, and for the young lady?"

"Well, I'll have the biggest burger you have, with everything on it." I say smiling at David, handing him the menu, then looking at my mom basically telling her, I got you.

"Right away ma'am thank you." David walked off with my menu, but not before he slid his number to me. I grab it and hide it in my purse under the table.

"Well, well, well, a young woman who knows what she wants. That is refreshing."

"What can I say Mr. Jones, if I want it at the moment why not take it, something I learned from my mother," he raises his glass as if I played the game well.

What seemed like a century went by; we were finally all ready to leave for the night. I guess I have to admit the evening wasn't all that bad and I quite enjoyed myself much more than I had expected.

"Eva, you are quite the commentator, you know how to lighten the mood." Mrs. Jones just laughed as we walked out of the restaurant.

"Calling it like I see it," my mother says as she is leaning up against Mrs. Jones hysterically laughing.

"It was a pleasure ladies thank you for joining us for lunch, I am sorry honey I must go. We shall see you tomorrow at 8 a.m. Paulina, thank you for joining us common folk with your presence, truly a pleasure." Mr. Jones reaches for my hand and gives it a kiss and gets in his own car to drive off.

"Yes, Paulina, you are a delightful treat. If you are not busy tomorrow maybe you can sit in on a business meeting, maybe it will come into some good use for you in the future."

"Oh unfortunately she won't be able to make it, she has already made plans with her best friend Deni. Isn't that right?"

I got the hint that my mother already did her good deed for the next few weeks so I shook it off and said, "This is true, thank you Mrs. Jones for everything and even the offer, I really would like to take in this city a bit more before I have to leave again, you know it will come in a blink of an eye."

"I definitely understand dear, go enjoy your break, you will miss them later."

"Yes, my mother had mentioned something similar to that earlier today."

"Very wise, she is. Well until tomorrow Eva, and until the party Ms. Paulina."

The car ride home was super quiet, pulling out my teeth seemed far less excruciating. "Thank you for not making yourself unpleasant to be around this afternoon." My mother says forcing a conversation let alone a compliment.

"I can say the same to you, your commentary was pretty funny though." I say looking towards her. Forcing a smile to crack to lighten up my compliment.

"Thank you, I would have to agree though, the menus were ridiculously a waste of having its own restaurant." We both just burst out laughing. Not long after our genuine moment did we pull up to the house. I was actually kind of bummed out because deep down this was something I needed, longed for, missed even. And then reality hit when my mom said, "I have to close another deal, probably won't be back until later on tonight."

"Yeah I get it," we both knew what kind of deal this would be. Involving a man and her drunk with nothing but sex on their minds. "Thanks for the dress and the lunch, I'll see you later." Ethan opens up the door and closes it. "Thank you Ethan."

"Here," he hands me a phone charger. "I thought your phone was dead and that is why I haven't received a single text message from you, so now I would hope to get something from you soon." He smiles at me, I couldn't help but chuckle.

"Thank you, I actually needed this, but why did you get me two chargers?"

"I wasn't sure if you are team Android or team Iphone."

"Ha, I guess you still won't know." He giggles as I walk away. He heads into the car and pulls off. I wish I would be the one to drive off with him, even if only for one night.

Chapter NINE

"HAHA, OH MY Ethan you are something else, I can't believe that is how you lost the state championship."

"Hey, now that word was very hard to spell for any 5th grader."

"Oh yes, the word petal has been known to be the big tripper upper of its kind."

"Well I should have asked for a definition, or maybe a sentence. I was so nervous, and shocked I even made it that far, I just froze."

"I have to hand it to you though, you manage to spell *pedal* correctly."

"Haha, I was hated by everyone, they stuffed the word petal with the letter t bold as well as flowers in my locker every single day for the rest of that school year."

"I am so sorry that you were bullied that year. Kids can be so cruel."

"The world is just cruel. Failure is not my fortune. It is all just a learning experience. We need to learn to not be afraid to ask, to get clarity for understanding and if we get it wrong then we simply get back up and try it again. Anyways, it is okay, everyone forgot about it over the summer and I hit puberty, everyone hardly even recognized me."

"Oh you became this big hot shot in school now?"

"I wouldn't say that, just because you have a big crowd around you all the time doesn't mean any of them are ever truly your friend, people want to be a part of the next big thing, so they cling on so when the next big thing happens they can say they were there all along. Yet, when things get rocky and change is the only thing that is inevitable to take place no matter how uncomfortable it may get people run away because they can't fathom the thought that it is not always

125

perfect here and everything has to take its own accountability."

Man, the way this man's brain is so mature and intellectual, I just can't help but want to fall in love, "Maybe we are all trying to belong and we are trying to find that place that is home."

"I agree, I guess my follow up is if we are all trying to belong and we get to what we believe is home how come we still trash our home? In the sense of turning against those we say are our family, hurting them because they hurt us, or we are envious of them. Maybe perhaps our motives aren't of any good intention as much as we want to perceive it to be, we say to people, ' you belong with us' because you are just like us and yet we still do wicked and evil things to one another and claim that they were never a part of us; either through words or action."

"I am not sure, life is just complicated. It is not all black and white."

"Maybe it was always meant to be, and this world is just a fallen kingdom that says a gray area is okay because it is even more colorful. I think it just brings destruction to those who we were always intended to love throughout our lives, being so graciously given, whether or not for a moment or til the end of our mortal time."

"So you say that the only time you are ever capable of loving is if it is fully unconditional no matter how much someone broke you, mistreated you?"

"Yes."

"How so?"

"At some point you loved that person, willingly to move all of creation for them no matter what and the moment they hurt you it is time to pick up the dagger of hate. I am not saying pain isn't real nor is how they mishandle your heart and feelings, I am saying that if you truly love someone you will always love them no matter what, you just don't have to be in love with them. Love is the ultimate opposite of hate, if hate has its conditions to generate towards someone how can love be in the same category? Then everything that is meant to be opposite through the building of this entire creation is intentionally all the equivalent and there is nothing that is opposite or the same if we are to believe that love and hate reside in the same house."

"Does not both have the parallelism of causing change? Are they not similar due to this result so perhaps they are both generated by conditions."

"Good question, they do cause change when someone experiences the effect of both, one for the better the other for the worse. We can either be in one cycle or the other until something else changes. Someone else comes along to question everything we thought we knew about either subject. Does not mean they are both generated by conditions, they are both daily choices made and yet only one outweighs the conditions, the one that is harder to take into consideration, a simple word that allows us to see past the bondage we want to cling on to; that is to understand."

"Understand?"

"If I understand that we are all trying to get through this life the best way we always thought, I can't take it personal. We are all constantly in a vicious cycle of this world, we learn what we have been through. So we teach that along to many generations, and to be honest it is hard for anyone to change their

mind set when their way of thinking all their years becomes interrupted and everything they thought they knew was certain is now demolished and that causes people to either run or go with it."

"So we can either be arrogant and stay in the pattern of hate or be willing to change to bring forth love. What if I say that I dislike someone and not necessarily hate them?"

"What is the difference to you?"

"Well hate is such a strong and forceful feeling compared to me just not liking someone."

"So a dislike is a more mild interpretation towards someone? I guess this is why the world established a middle ground to make it seem like it is okay, here is where we come into that gray area again. There is two negatives that is the same no matter how much we could debate on how they are different because at the end of it, it is all based on a condition of what someone did or didn't do to us, love is not a forceful feeling, it is an inviting feeling that is welcoming and yet holds so much power. If I could choose, I'd rather be inviting and hold power instead of being strong and forceful."

The way he said that sent shivers down my spine, so gentle and yet you can tell he knows who he is with knowing there is authority and truth in what he says. "I can't believe it is after 3 in the morning, we have been talking on this phone for hours."

"I thought we were trying to make it two days in a row where we talk all night long."

"That was my goal, I really do enjoy talking to you, I guess like you said some people get scared when their way of thinking gets altered."

"I don't believe that I said people get scared, I do get it though. Does that mean you will run away or go with it."

"I guess we will find out."

"Paulina wake up, wake up, wake up."

"Deni, leave me alone, let me sleep for a few more hours." I tell her as she is jumping on my bed.

"A few more hours? Girl it is 4 o'clock in the afternoon, you've been sleeping all day. Did you forget it is Christmas Eve, meaning the big party your mother is hosting at the Jones'."

"Oh great" I hurry and pull back he covers, "I totally forgot that was today, I was up all night."

"Yeah you have been exhausted a lot lately and kind of glowing too, who did you sleep with? Tell me all the dirty deets."

"Not everyone glows after sex Deni," I say, snapping at her.

"Oh dang, okay. I am sorry, I am just curious as to what has been going on."

"I'm sorry I shouldn't have been snapping at you, I have been talking to Ethan all week over the phone and the past couple of nights we don't get done talking until 6 in the morning."

"Dang! Look at you getting at mister sexy pants."

"Don't talk about him like that, he is more than just a piece of meat. He is so different and he should be treated as such."

"I feel like someone is in love."

Me in love, is that even possible? What has this man done to me, after our big conversation last night about love and change did that get to me? Did that make me start questioning everything I ever knew. I am not sure how I actually feel about this. "Nonsense Deni, we know I am not capable of that. I can't love any man."

"Are you capable of loving anyone?"

"I love you, always."

"Is it love if it is just me? Isn't love supposed to spread around, no matter what?"

I stopped in my tracks as I was getting ready. What was Deni trying to get at?

Ring, Ring

"It's your mother."

"Ugh, what does this woman want?" I hurry and run to the phone to pick it up. "Yes, mother?"

"Where are you, you were supposed to be here early to help me with the set up."

"I was sleeping, shouldn't I have my beauty sleep?"

"Well I guess you will need plenty of it. You know what I don't care, you better be here by 8, if not you can kiss any college tuition from me goodbye. If you want to deliberately ruin my night then I'll ruin your future." She quickly hangs up before I could even say anything.

"Ugh, she is such a monster Deni, how could anyone love her?"

"Your dad did."

I look at Deni with a sharp look, then I soften it. I couldn't help but think about the word understanding. Yes, it seems so unfair that my mom would ruin my future over one night, and yet I know it is more than just a night, it is her future. Dang Ethan. I grab my towel and head for the shower trying to escape.

Knock, Knock

"Lina? Hey my mom called me and I am needed to go help finish setting up. I will see you at the party, okay?"

"Okay Deni. I'll see you soon."

———————

That wasn't the real conversation that Deni had and that wasn't her mom on the phone.

"Hello?"

"You said you had some important news to share with me?" A dark strange voice is on the other side, completely intrigued and impatient.

"Yes my love, she seems to be falling for someone who is making a huge impact on her. So much so that it seems like your plans will get ruined."

"What?! I want you to destroy whatever bond they have by any means necessary. If not, don't bother coming back to me."

"Yes, I understand."

"Oh darling, don't sound so sad. I couldn't ever just throw you out that quickly."

"Thank you."

"For now."

———————

As I got out of the shower the steam couldn't help but fog up the mirror. Covering up my reflection. I swiped the mirror to see myself and I quickly regretted it. I didn't like who I saw in the mirror so I rushed out of the bathroom. I wish I could bring the steam back to fill up the bathroom all over again so I didn't have to see myself due to uncertainty of who I am. Unfortunately I was in the shower for so long that I wasted all the hot water. I slowly get ready, dreading to even go and thinking of Ethan the entire time.

Wanting to be in his arms, to hear his voice, and to find home in his eyes. The doorbell rings causing me to break free from my thought process.

"Come in!" I yell out down the staircase. Not knowing if whoever was at the door even heard me.

"Paulina?"

Well there is my answer. "Ethan?"

"I was ordered to come pick you up to take you to Mr. and Mrs. Jones house for the party."

"I am almost done. I'll be down in a sec."

"Don't worry, take your time."

I finished putting on my earrings and heels. And walk out of the room headed to the top of the staircase. Ethan was at the bottom looking right up at me, in complete awe. He looked at me as if this world couldn't compare to my existence. His eyes were lit up and glossed over, they were like a passionate flame and I felt as if I were like coals burning in the pressure of the heat, I was nothing but a diamond in his eyes.

"Paulina, nothing in all creation is as beautiful as you, you are the crown of all beauty."

I couldn't help but blush as I reached the end of the staircase looking at him, feeling every word he said forming every inch of my body. "Thank you Ethan. I thought my beauty wasn't measured by my wardrobe choice." He grabs my coat and purse and puts it on me. He leads me to the mirror by the door, alluring me to look into the mirror.

"Your beauty has always been from the inside, the presence of royalty has

137

always been within you. Right now at this moment you are just walking in it. Confident in you, not in anything this world temporarily offers."

As I stared into the mirror, hesitant and all, struggling to really see myself. I turned away from the mirror trying to hold back my tears and I looked at him.

"What is wrong?"

"I feel so naked and ashamed of who I am"

He brings me in close, tightening his grip with his arms around me. Not afraid to confront the battle I placed before him, seeing me. "You don't need to feel ashamed when you are with me. The only exposure I want from you is the fullness of your heart. However that may look." I lean in and kiss him. He grabs the back of my neck gently and ever so intensely kisses me back. The heat between us two was suffocating me and yet every kiss was giving me life. A tear left my eyes, for the first time, I never felt so alive. Like a rainbow at the end of a storm, like a garden becoming in bloom. The tear was more than a tear. "Are you okay?" He asked me as he felt the tear-drop fall on him.

"Yes I am, I.." my phone rings inter-rupting what me and Ethan were sharing with one another. "Hello?"

"I hope you are on your way, it is almost 8."

"Yes mother I am on my way I'll be there." I hang up the phone and look at Ethan. "We better go."

"As you wish." Getting into the car I couldn't help but look out the window and reminisce about the few seconds Ethan and I had. Those few seconds felt like a lifetime with him. Time does not exist when I am with him, how is this even possible. I want to spend every living, breathing moment with him. Of course there are other things that get in the way that causes me to have to leave his side. Time to head into Mr. and Mrs. Jones' home. But to my surprise, right on the dot my mother swings the door open and says,

"There you are Paulina, come on in, you are so lucky you made it here on time. Now let's go, we need to make an impression on these fine guests. Oh and no sas tonight."

"Yes." I enter the Jones' mansion, "Wow, do you think someone is compensating."

"Paulina!"

"Sorry, no sas."

"Go in and mingle as if you didn't just get here. I need to make sure everyone stays satisfied."

"Well you shouldn't have a problem with that, since you are so good at it." Before my mother could snap back with something hurtful to say I heard my name being called from behind me.

"Paulina, I am so glad you are here," my mother's sharp look said enough; that if I said one more thing she was about to cut all life support. I turn around and I see Mr. Jones walking towards us. "Eva, so far everything is splendid, I have some colleagues who are dying to know who put this magnificent party together, come with me. Paulina please help yourself to anything in this house, go enjoy." Mr. Jones takes my mother by the hips, guiding her back to the party. As he walks and talks with her he looks back at me giving me a look that said, "*later.*"

I go and join the rest of the party, looking for Deni. Where could she be? As I am walking and snatching up some hors d'oeuvres I couldn't help but notice many conversations and interactions. Mrs. Jones kept running to the bathroom a lot. I am not sure why she broke the seal. At the same time she hardly touched her drink. I thought it was a bit shady so I went on a mission. I followed her up to the bedroom and I could hear whispers. "Oh, Matt. Please don't stop."

"Patricia, you feel so amazing. Tell me whose it is."

"You know it's yours, my husband hasn't touched this in years." I couldn't help and be shocked that I ran down the hall as quickly as I could.

"Lina?" I hear a voice behind me, completely scared of who it could be. I turn around and I see Deni.

"Deni, where have you been all night? I haven't seen you since I've been here."

"I was having phone sex with Zared."

"For 3 hours?"

"This man knows his words, he takes foreplay to a whole other level."

"Okay, too much information."

"Since when? Are you okay? You look like you have seen a ghost."

I saw something die of course, a marriage. "Yeah I am fine, just need to sip on a drink to make this party a bit more bearable."

"I am way ahead of you, look at what I brought in," she pulls out a bottle of Vodka. We head into the nearest bathroom and start taking shots like there was no tomorrow.

"You know I saw Mrs. Jones getting it on with some random dude in the bedroom before I ran into you."

"No way! Mrs. Jones a horny junkie? I would have never guessed. Is Mr. Jones not hitting it right?"

"Apparently he isn't hitting it at all."

"What no way, how do you know that?"

"That is what she was moaning about."

"Dang, so who is Mr. Jones hooking up with?"

"I am not sure, what if he is faithful here."

"Yeah right, did you see how fine that man is, he can close a business deal on me any day." We both started laughing.

"Yes! That man stays in shape for sure he can bench press me any day, any position, anywhere multiple times."

We continued laughing unapologetically stumbling out of the bathroom and our laughter turned into fear. "Paulina, Deni have we been drinking?" Looking at us with his hands behind his back standing tall with one eyebrow raised, intrigued to what our response would be.

"Mr. Jones! Uh, we just thought we could enjoy ourselves a little bit, we are young after all." I say hoping that he didn't hear anything outside this door.

"Deni, your mother is looking for you, she is ready to leave."

"Yes, Mr. Jones, thank you for the lovely party." Deni looks at me and walks away. As she is walking, she turns around and starts making an invisible blow job and fake sex pounding behind Mr. Jones basically telling me to get it on with that man.

"Well, I must get back to the party before someone notices I wasn't mingling with the guests."

Mr. Jones reaches for my hand, "I suggest we go try and sober you up a bit before your mother sees and loses her cool." As much as I wasn't really in the right mind space to care I knew deep down he was right, I saw how hard my mom worked on this party and as much as we didn't get along it wasn't right for me to go out of my way to intentionally ruin her night. I did after all tell her I'd be on my best behavior.

"You are right Mr. Jones"

"Please call me Eric, right this way, I have some coffee heating up in my office." We head into his office in the far off corner of his mansion. "Take a seat I'll grab you a cup of coffee, any cream or sugar?"

"Yes please," he hands me the cup of coffee, "thank you, Eric."

"You sound so mature when you say my name."

"I believe I look pretty mature too." Eric clears his throat, blushing and turns away. Walking over to the other couch in his office. "I am not a little girl anymore, you can look at me as a woman." I stood up heading over to him as he stretched himself out. I get on top of him starting to kiss him on his lips, then his neck and he moans.

"Paulina..."

"Call me Lina."

"Okay, Lina, what are you doing?"

"Are you really asking me this question? I know you want it as much as I do."

"You know I heard your little remarks in the bathroom with Deni, you want me to bench press you." As he says this he pulls my hips closer to where I can feel everything that was him, I couldn't tell where it begins and where it ends. I couldn't help but let out a moan. "I can press myself fully into you, if that is what you want." Eric grabs my neck firmly and starts bringing me in closer and starts kissing my neck, licking and blowing at the same time practically writing his name with his tongue all over my chest. His hands begin to go inside of me and I start rubbing him with a firm enough grip letting him know I am in control. We were breathing heavily kissing one another, then I felt a sense of emptiness as we were kissing.

"Paulina?" I turned around so fast to see who said my name.

"Ethan?" I jumped off of Eric quickly, but Ethan was already long gone before my feet hit the ground. I stopped in the doorway with tears streaming down my face. How could I do what I just did, as I am standing in the doorway Mrs. Jones and my mother were coming up the hallway, looking at me confused.

"Lina," Eric says, coming after me buckling up his pants."

"Eric! What is going on?"

"Patricia, she came onto me, trying to sweeten me up so that I would make sure I talked well on your behalf, Eva."

"What?!" My mother says hurt.

"Yeah What?!" I say. "I didn't do it so you can get my mother jobs."

"So you initiated contact with my husband?"

"Well yes, I.."

"Wow, get out of my house Paulina. Eva please follow right behind her. I will make sure the rest of the evening closes without you."

"Patricia," my mother says with such a sad voice, completely shattered.

"Please just go Eva." My mother looks at me and then growls walking away swiftly.

"You have a lot of nerve Patricia," I say angrily, "does your precious husband know about Matt?"

"How dare you, Paulina." Before she had the chance to continue speaking I walked away.

"Really Eric," Patricia says, "you just couldn't keep it in your pants when it came to her, you just had to have her."

Eric looks at her fiercely and takes his two fingers and sucks on them, smiles and walks away, "Mmm, if you don't mind I need to go finish," he says as he shuts his office door.

"Mother, wait, it's not what you think."

"What, my daughter thought I couldn't do a good enough job on my own so she felt the need to sleep with my boss. Or how about that my daughter hates me so much she wanted to ruin any part of my dream that felt alive, real, worth having after so many years." She grabs on her coat and rushes to the car. Ethan standing there with frozen tears streaming down his face. He opens the door for my mother. I grab my coat and purse and run after my mom, I couldn't have her think I was a monster. Ethan opens the door for me.

"Mom, I am so sorry. I wasn't thinking. I did a stupid thing. You should know a lot about that."

"Are you serious Paulina? You are trying to apologize to me by trying to bring up all the crap I've done. I know I have made horrible decisions in the past, I am trying to do something for myself for the first time and you want to get in the way of that. You are such an ungrateful spoiled brat. That is all your father's fault."

"How dare you talk about dad like that, he is the only one that cared about me. You only cared about his money and when that ran out you decided to bang the whole neighborhood to move on from him quickly." She slaps me across the face.

"You have no idea what I have faced trying to provide after his death so that his final wishes for you to prosper came true. Nor do you have any right to tell me about banging my problems away, clearly that apple didn't fall too far from the tree."

"Ethan, stop the car."

"Ma'am?"

"Ethan you heard my daughter, if she wants to get out of this car while it is snowing let it be."

"As you wish ma'am." He stops the car and I get out. As I see the car drive off and make that right at the stop sign I walk and make that left. I pull out my phone and I start scrolling to see who to call.

*Ring, Ring *

"Cypher, are you still in Colorado?"

"I sure am, I am at a strip club, if you want to come through I'll send you the address."

"I'm on my way."

Cypher: 1010 Shallow Lane, Durango Colorado. Tempus Voluptas. See you then sexy ;)

It felt like this walk took forever to the nearest noticeable place for the Uber driver to come pick me up from. Everything was running through my mind all the way to the strip club. I needed a drink, I needed some weed, heck I needed Cypher to get my mind off of everything that just happened. Finally pulling up to this strip club, it looked well put together on the outside, I could only imagine the inside despite my personal opinion about what this place really was. I never thought I would see myself here.

"Excuse me miss, what is your name?"

"Oh, I was invited by a friend. I'm sure you can let me in."

"Sorry ma'am there is a private party going on in there. I need a name in order to see if you are on the list."

"Lina Saville."

"I see you are one of the dancers, go ahead."

"Thank you," what does he mean by dancer?

I walk in and see half naked girls everywhere, many rooms with curtains and people having pleasure left and right. Not caring of who may be watching. I am looking everywhere to find Cypher.

"Excuse me miss, you are needed in the deluxe suite."

"Me?" The gentleman nods as he leads me up the stairs and into a room that seems to have a glass window all around it hovering the strip club. You could see everything. There is a pole in the middle of the room with its own bar, pool, and bed.

"Here you are miss, the boss will be with you."

"Boss?" he shuts the door and I start searching around, what is this room? Why am I up here? Maybe I can see where Cypher is. I couldn't help but think about what just happened. This big spacious building reminded me of Mr. and Mrs. Jones mansion. They were compensating for something, the lack of heart they truly had for one another. They put on a show of how much in love they are when all along they could care less.

"Are you going to just stand over there or are you going to start dancing for me?" I turned around to see who was talking and it was Cypher. I run up to him and start to kiss him. "Woah," he says, pushing me away. "I mean what I say, you came here to a strip club, so go and dance or else you can just leave. I am here to enjoy a bachelor's party."

"What? Speaking of that, who is the man getting married?"

"No one, there was a possessive statement in that; meaning any eligible bachelor who wants to have a good time, marriage isn't my thing, you should know that."

"Oh, so you own this place?"

"Okay, I'll bite for a second. Yes I am the owner, how do you think you got in as a dancer? Speaking of that," he reaches for the phone, "yeah, Ricky bring me up Kinky Kiki." Hanging up the phone he looks at me in a darkish way.

"Are you serious, I came here to be with you and you want to call up another woman."

Throwing back his drink he places the shot glass down. Walking towards me feeling the heat long before he ever grabbed me. Leaning me into the bar, he starts to kiss me caressing my thighs and my butt, squeezing so tight that super glue would be considered the generic brand. "You may make it hard, but if you want to witness me cumming then you need to be a good girl and do what I tell you to do."

Kiki walks in, gets on the pole and starts dancing. Cypher looks at me, grabs my hand and places it on his junk and starts rubbing it. Looking sternly in my eyes he says, "The choice is yours but make it quick, I'm not a very patient man." As he sits down on the couch watching

Kiki dance he pays me no mind, as if I am not even there. I start to walk away, why would I stay here if he doesn't even notice me, and before I could reach the door knob that same thought was the exact reason why I didn't leave, I couldn't help but not to be seen by him, if he wanted to see a show, he will get all that plus an encore. I drop my jacket on the floor and start walking up to the pole, giving Kiki the look to walk away, she looks at Cypher waiting for permission of what he wanted her to do. As I squat low looking at him and he looks at me, he looks back at her and gives her the signal to leave the room with his head. As I am still dancing on the pole he starts to rub on himself and smiles not looking away, and that is exactly what I wanted. I start to walk over to him and start dancing on him, he slowly starts taking off my dress. Kissing me as I move up against him. As I am sitting on him he takes his tie off and grabs my wrists placing them behind my back, he pushes me up and takes me over to the bar and leans me over. Tying my hands behind my back he then spreads my legs and removes my underwear and gives me the most intense oral pleasure I had ever received. Then he slowly started licking back up. What seemed like forever I couldn't feel his touch, from any part of his body, and then out of nowhere he entered into me such a shock came over me I inhaled so deeply, hyperventilating trying to catch my breath.

Chapter TEN

"5...4...3...2...1 HAPPY NEW YEAR!" Deni yells while grabbing hold of me. "This is our year Lina!"

"Sure is!" We click our shots together and throw it back. Is it really my year? I haven't talked to my mother since Christmas Eve.

Ethan: Happy New Year Paulina.

As for Ethan I haven't responded to any of his messages. How can I face him after the heartbreak I caused him. How do I know he isn't going to yell at me and shame me because he caught me in the act of doing something so stupid, and with a married man. What does he think of me?

"Lina, stop looking at your phone, come be in this moment with me."

"Yeah, you are right." I put my phone away still leaving another message unresponded.

Deni and I started to let loose on the dance floor. As I was trying to dance and drink my heartache and pain away nothing seemed to heal this golf size hole in my chest. I started to feel dizzy and queasy not only because I was twisted but also because there seemed no hope to overcome or be redeemed from everything that had happened. Mainly to what I did to Ethan and yes even my mother. She may not be the easiest woman to get along with but playing back what she said of how she had to make decisions to fulfill my dad's final wishes makes me think of how there is probably more than what I've seen to know. It's like an iceberg. How we only see the tip of the iceberg not realizing there is the rest of it under the surface that is still left to uncover. To not jump into judgment of how someone else is acting without getting to know why they are hurting, where they are hurting.

Aren't we all trying to figure out the crazy life that we live in? Such a chaotic world this is. Trying to understand how to survive every day knowing what we know what to do and how to do it just to get by. Yes even though they are hurting, it doesn't mean they should lash out their hurt on anyone else... maybe I need to take my own advice on that. At some point we need to take accountability for ourselves of how to treat people, also I probably should start to find healing within myself. Where? How? When I do, I want to share that. Especially if I can pass that healing to someone else, what is the point of receiving healing and not ever sharing that healing? How could I be so cold hearted, dead like a corpse knowing there are so many people who are hurting just like me and I have the secret to a hope filled life healed and restored. Why would I want to keep that to myself? How could I say I love people or want to help them out, especially since I am going to be a counselor.

"Lina! Girl there is some hottie checking you out, go and do your thing." I glance over in the direction Deni was pointing to and I see this tall stranger smiling from ear to ear, raising his glass to show that we are both making that mutual contact.

"Oh, he is very handsome, but I don't think so tonight Deni, I am not feeling too well. I think I am just going to leave."

"Are you sure? You know he would be more than willing to leave with you."

"I am sure, I will call you later."

"Okay, sounds good. Do you want me to call for an Uber?"

"No I am just going to walk, the fresh air would be great, plus I am staying only a couple blocks away from here." I gave Deni a hug and kissed her on her cheek. I grabbed my coat and started to head for the door. I finally reached outside, it felt like the longest walk of my life to finally breathe. As I took in that fresh air, finding some sanity in the craziness that had seemed to be all around me, I knew that this walk was only temporary. It didn't compare to the longer walk that was going on in my head, that road and darkness matched the night sky. I don't like this feeling. Abandoned with only the negative thoughts to 'comfort' me. I started to feel anxious. Maybe I should go back to the party and leave with that guy, so I don't have to be here alone with these tormenting thoughts. As I turned around I realized I was so lost in my thoughts that I actually was lost. "Where is my phone?" I started to ask out loud.

"Ha, ha, ha" a voice echoing in the dark.

"Who is there?" I say with a quiver in my voice.

"You will be his," one voice says

"Yes, you can't escape from him," another voice says, all echoing still.

"How dare you think you can run away from your decisions"

"So pathetic"

"LEAVE ME ALONE! Why don't you show yourself and stop being a coward," I screamed!

"A coward?" laughing and mocking.

"You are a coward"

"Yeah a coward who doesn't know who she is," the laughing and mocking were all unforgiving, echoing into the night.

"Yeah, you are never going to be enough for anyone."

"Such a shy and timid little girl. What are you going to do?"

"No one loves you, not even your mother"

I started to run away, there were so many voices that I knew I couldn't take on whoever was after me. As I started to run I slid on the ice and broke my foot. I tried to get up but there was nothing that I could grab on to in order to give myself leverage. From a far off distance I could see a tree, I started to crawl to the tree, using every inch of panic and fear to motivate me enough to keep pushing forward no matter how cold and hurt I was. Yet, that wasn't enough to keep me going, with all the booze and the emotions running through me. I could only see the tree fading away, questioning if it's existence was even there in the first place. Then a light seemed to shine on me, it felt warm and yet I couldn't help but drift away into the darkness still.

Going in and out of consciousness I could hear someone talking over me, machines beeping all around.

"She has a severe injury on her left leg, somehow it was broken, placed back together and then re-broken. She has some severe scratches on her arms. So deep that it almost looks like an animal attacked her. And she has some mild damage in her left eye, whoever did this to her was aiming to torture her, causing enough pain to get a message across."

"Do you have any reason to believe someone would intentionally do this to her? Or is this some kind of accident?"

"I believe someone was aiming for her sir," a stern yet compassionate voice speaks up. Why does that voice sound so familiar?

"Good thing you found her when you did, if her open wounds took any more of that freezing cold weather she wouldn't have made it." I heard a hard sigh with feet walking away from me, Next thing I knew the door had shut.

"Wh... wh... where am I?" I ask in a groggy voice barely seeing out of the one eye I had available to me.

"Shh, Ms. Saville, you are at the hospital. My name is Doctor James Arlo. You have been in a crazy incident and your injuries are in critical condition. We have tried to contact your mother but she has not answered the phone."

"Don't bother trying to get in touch with her, she doesn't care enough about me to come."

"I'm sure that isn't true. I will keep reaching her. I will bring the nurse in here to check in on you."

Arlo? Why does that last name sound so familiar? My head was hurting too much to keep thinking so I waited patiently for the nurse to come in while the doctor checked a couple machines and took some notes then went on his way.

"Hello, Ms. Saville; I am Nurse Dorothy Johnson. I will be your nurse in the morning and then Nurse Phil Taylor will be your evening nurse for the duration of your stay. We will be coming in every other hour to make sure vitals are still good and to administer any medication the doctor feels is needed for you. We will also be here anytime you need us to help you to the bathroom, just push this red button on the side here and it will notify us immediately. We are your personal nurses so we won't ever be too busy for you."

"Why because there aren't enough patients here that need assistance? Or is it because of who my mother is?"

"No ma'am," she responds back softly, looking at me with such a sincere heart, "because you are in need of assistance and our primary goal is to make sure you are taken care of. Every patient here who needs to stay here for a full day or more gets their own personal nurses, while other nurses help attend with those who don't need to stay here any longer than a day. It is quite a fulfilling job because we don't have to make anyone feel rushed or left out. We all attend accordingly and with the utmost care and compassion just like Doctor James Arlo would like. It is a very thought out organization filled with such purpose."

"So is this doctor like your boss?"

"He is the owner of this hospital."

"The owner? Why doesn't he go relax on a beach somewhere and let other doctors take care of this place. Early retirement?"

"Oh no ma'am, he loves what he does and he loves the many people who come seeking help here. He wants nothing but the best for everyone that comes in, even if patients don't agree with what he gives them because they are seeking something else, they leave satisfied everytime and thank him for knowing that they were given a longer lasting result. He is more than willing to help people get on the same page of his will and purpose. And if they aren't he must let them go."

"So what, he doesn't give them another chance?"

"He gives many chances, it is up to those who want to work here or even be a patient here to be willing to understand his view and mission in his divine plan. Now if you are a part of his administration team that is a different story."

"So basically it's his way or the highway? How does that seem right, what if there are others that come in with a good idea to expand the business? Why is the administration team different?"

"It's not necessarily the highway, he is more than willing to work with others and he has the brains and the power to put into place the idea to expand on his own. Most of the time when people bring ideas they tend to give them so they themselves be exalted, glorified, king, etc. to divide what Doctor James Arlo created here. What he has going on here is like perfection in a cup and he is wanting to pour that cup into other hospitals. He is always working and moving to expand outside of these four walls. The administration team is to make sure that his plan is to be set into place and they are usually the ones who want the authority all to themselves and if they have the slightest thought of only caring for themselves and their pockets they jeopardize the very essence of what he has to offer here and he would be no different from any other place here in this world. He wants to be different from the status quo. He wants real results and more people to see that there is actual help, hope and peace here."

"Oh, okay. I apologize for my quick judgment."

"It's okay Ms. Saville. You didn't know, therefore you didn't understand but now you do and the fact that you were willing to apologize and see; we can move forward in doing better and what is right."

"What is right?"

"Getting all the information before persecuting someone else for their decisions." She walks out with a smile on her face that was so warm and tender. There was no guilt for me to ponder on. I felt like I was free from my accusation against the doctor.

Knock, Knock

"Come in," who is knocking at my door? Was it my mother? Were they able to reach her, did she care and love me enough to come check up on me, did she forgive me?

"Hello, Paulina."

"Ethan? You are here? Why?"

Holding flowers and wearing a faint smile he comes in and shuts the door. "I just wanted to check up on you and make sure you were okay." He had so much sadness in his eyes. He looked the way I felt, as if we were in sync with each other. I could see how heartbroken he was to see me this way. Like he was completely shattered that this happened to me.

"I'm okay, just in some pain."

"I brought you these flowers, do you mind if I set them down over here on this table?"

"Not at all, thank you for them, they look beautiful. Surprising that I can see that with one eye covered huh?"

"Well good thing you were made with two eyes or else it just would have been more shocking then surprising."

We start chuckling at his attempt to make everything seem okay. And for a moment it felt like everything was going to be okay. Him just being here seemed to make all the pain go away, inside and out and I didn't want him to leave. And from my conversation earlier with Nurse Dorothy I knew I needed to apologize once and for all to Ethan. To stop running away with my guilt and shame. "Ethan?"

"Yes Paulina?"

He was just staring into me, like he already knew what I was going to say because the look on his face showed me the answer I was longing and waiting for.

Tears started to stream down my face. "I am so sorry. I am sorry for hurting you. I am sorry for not valuing what we were starting to have. I decided to go chase after another man, a married man at that. I am sorry that I chose to be a part of an adulterous life. Please, please, please forgive me. I will do anything for your forgiveness. I can't keep running from my pain and the pain I have caused. Please..."

He comes running up to me holding me tight as I am just weeping into his arms. He leans in and whispers in my ear, "I forgave you the moment that it happened. You don't have to beg for my forgiveness nor do anything to earn it. I graciously give it to you because I love you, Paulina. The best apology is a changed behavior."

"You love me? Why were you crying that night while you were waiting for me?"

"I was crying because I was hurt; because of the betrayal, but I was also hurt because you felt the need that you had to do what you did. So my tears were for you because you must have been hurt and in a lot of pain to put yourself in such a situation and I couldn't help but want to understand and show my compassion. Yes, I love you and I always will, nothing and no one can change that."

"You don't know how awful I have been and all the horrible things I have done. You don't know me. I am not worthy or even enough to receive this kindness, grace and mercy from you." He drops his arms and sits on the bed taking my hand in his, not losing any eye contact.

"Says who, you? If we go around this life never wanting to receive a free gift from someone else, especially in the time of needing it, then we will never truly appreciate anything ever given to us in our lives. We are our biggest critics and because of that it opens a door for others to criticize and we start listening to their opinions and thoughts about us and when they seem to align with what we were already thinking about ourselves in such a negative way we start to call it truth. Let someone who is willing to do anything for you, even lay down their life for you to define how important, special, worthy and valuable you are. Not someone who is passing through to cause you to stumble out of their own dark and twisted motives."

I sat there taking in everything Ethan was saying. It made so much sense. I didn't know how to process or even respond and so all I said was, "Please keep holding me and love me unconditionally."

"Yesterday and forever I vow I will."

Chapter ELEVEN

"GOOD MORNING MS. SAVILLE. I hope you got plenty of rest here and that you have felt comfortable."

"Yes, I sure did Doctor Arlo. Arlo? Arlo! You are Ehan's father aren't you?"

Doctor James is checking the charts and starts to laugh hysterically. "Yes ma'am Ethan is my son. He is the reason you are here. He found you in a pit. Speaking of that, do you remember what happened that night? You have some serious injuries here."

"I barely remember anything."

"Well can you tell me what you remember, even if it is not in chronological order."

"Umm okay," Doctor James started to remove my bandage over my eye and took his retinoscope and started to shine it over. I heard my heartbeat jumping around on the monitor.

"What do you see," He asked calmly.

"I remember seeing a light shining on me."

"Yes, that's good. What else?"

As he asked that, my mind flashed back into the night of my accident. "I saw a tree, it was hazy. Then it went dark. I heard voices."

"What were they saying?"

"Umm, they were saying that I deserve this punishment for all the pain I've caused. They brought up the names of guys I have slept with and dumped. They also brought up my mother and Ethan. And, and… Ahhh!!!" I scream and shake the memory away.

"Nurse, get in here now! Paulina look at me, it's okay. You aren't there any more. You don't live there anymore. Look at me please." As tears are streaming down my face, I finally get the courage to look at him. "Can you tell me what you saw that made you scream?"

"I, I can't. It's too painful."

"Okay, I understand. Holding it in will only cause you to keep replaying it in your head. My advice: if you do, keep seeing past the horrible moment, you then will see the good in it all."

"How is that possible Doc! Look at me I am beaten up, I was found in a pit, I haven't heard from my supposed best friend, my mother wants nothing to do with me. And taking a look at my leg I may not ever be able to walk again. An impossible situation to find anything good or even hopeful."

"It's okay to be angry and let out what is going on in your life. Just don't stay in your anger to where you start to believe that nothing good could ever happen again when in fact a lot of good passes you by. Like for instance you are alive being well taken care of, surrounded by people who are around the clock trying to get you strong and healthy again to get you up on your two feet. And if you don't appreciate their love and kindness then maybe you can at least see the love my son has for you."

I froze in what Doctor James was telling me. His wisdom pierced through not only my flesh but my soul and he made so much sense that I couldn't be angry anymore not even with him. The way he talked to me with authority and compassion. "Hey, Doctor James?"

"Yes Paulina?"

"You said that your son is the one who saved me and found me in a pit and brought me out. Can you tell me how?"

"I would, but I think it is better if you ask him yourself. Open up to him, trust him. I know it will be hard at first, but has he personally given you a reason not to trust him and to restrict him from knowing you and loving you."

"I guess you are right. Hey! One more thing before you leave. I noticed you were checking all my wounds including my leg. Do you think there is hope in restoring my leg to be brand new again."

"With me I can heal you back to brand new, if you are willing to put in the work, no matter how hard it will be. If you were to go anywhere else they would leave you in crutches followed by temporary medication to numb the pain away. If you deal with the pain head on you will no longer be in pain and no more crutches that the rest of the world would like to offer. Are you willing to accept and believe that I can do this for you?"

As he was staring into my eyes I knew that I wanted a change, that I wanted to get better. So I am willing to trust him and believe in what he was saying just enough to say, "Yes."

"Good, oh by the way the vision test we gave you for your left eye seems to show that you are back to normal. The amount of impact you have had on your eye was really extreme, good to know that your eye will be fine, it is still a bit bruised and you will still have to wear your glasses," he chuckles as if he was trying to make a joke. "In an hour we are going to get you on your feet, we are starting some physical therapy. Your leg is healing quite well from the damage it went through."

"Thank you Doctor James, for taking such good care of me even when I don't deserve it."

"Your well being is my priority, if I felt like you deserved my attention then I would base that off of what you have and have not done. As if it were being owed to you. Your life is not based on how many gold stars you get in your life; instead taking care of you is more of a reward for the fact that you are someone who was created for purpose and love. I shouldn't base my character off of what you are owed, deserved especially in the time of your healing and you trying and willingly to get better. Can we give each other some grace?" He smiles and walks out the door.

As he was gone I couldn't help but think of everything he was saying and I couldn't help but think about Ethan. How did he find me?

"Paulina, Paulina!" A woman yelling with tears in her voice crashed through my door.

"Mom!" Tears are streaming down my cheeks. "I didn't think you would come."

"What!? Of course I would come, honey you are my daughter, I love you no matter what."

"Even after what happened during Christmas. Mom I need you to know I was drunk and Eric was there and one thing led to another it had nothing to do with you. I promise there was no secret motive, I..."

"Paulina, please stop. I know you didn't do that to intentionally hurt me. I forgive you. Please forgive me for blaming you in ruining my career before it even took off and for slapping you, that was totally uncalled for. Please forgive me."

"Of course, you are my mama. Why did it take you so long to come here?"

"Oh, honey I was in Costa Rica. I was on the plane when everything happened to you. And I had a horrible reception.

Then when I was able to get access to some Wi-Fi with decent reception some dude who was totally wasted decided it would be funny to grab my phone from my hand and take selfies and it flew out of his hand into the ocean. Look at the backup photos on my new phone of this guy." She shows me on her phone how crazy she looked chasing after him and the big grin on his face and the 'uh-no' face on everybody. "I would have still been there if Ethan didn't come get me." She looks over in the doorway and Ethan is just standing there leaning over smiling at me. I didn't notice him coming in when my mom did. I was so focused on her. Oh how he looked so handsome, just standing in there being my hero every-where I turn. "I will be here everyday to check up on you and I will get your room ready for when you can officially come home." She says, making my gaze get off of Ethan, remembering that my mother was still in the room, watching her walk back and forth.

"Thank you for that mama, but I will need to get back to school at some point, the Spring semester has already started. Thankfully I reached out to my professors and told them the condition of my status and they are willing to record the lectures and I can watch them to get my assignments done. I guess that's what happens when you do so well in school."

"Good! Why do I feel like there is a 'but' in there somewhere?"

"Well, when I get the okay from the doctor to go back to school, that is my plan. Just letting you know mom."

"I understand."

"Knock, Knock" Doctor James enters the room. "Ethan, nice to see you and you are?"

"Eva Saville, Paulina's mother."

"Well hello there Eva. I just came in to update Paulina here on her progression. Paulina, your leg is recovering quite well. I am bumping our session three times a week. The fact that the tissue is not infected or even overlapping in any way is miraculous. Your bruise on your eye has gone down and your scratches have become scars. The stitching went very well. It has been a pleasure in going through this process with you. With that being said I will give you your release forms, you may leave tomorrow morning. I also come with some more news, with the injuries you have inquired and the way you came into my hospital I did have to report it to the proper authorities. Now I have kept them away as long as I can. They will be in shortly to ask you some questions."

"I understand, thank you for everything Doctor James."

"My pleasure." He walks out of the room waiving in for two police officers to enter the room.

"Hello Ms. Saville, Mrs. Saville, and you are?"

"Arlo, Ethan Arlo."

"Well Mr. Arlo, this is a private matter, your presence is not needed." Ethan staring down the two officers with his arms crossed showing them he was not moving anywhere.

"It's okay Ethan, I got it thank you." I told him to assure him that I was fine."

"Okay, but if you need me then let me know. I will be right outside this door." He leaves the room and closes the door right behind him.

"Ms. Saville, we are just here to ask you a few questions about the night of your accident."

"Okay."

"My name is Detective Roland and this is Detective Garcia. Can you tell us anything that happened on the night of your accident? Like the Day? Events leading up to it? What do you remember during it?"

"Well it was New Years Eve, well New Years Day when I left the party."

"What party?"

"It was a party that my friend Deni found through one of her mutual friends."

"Deni, is she still here?"

"No, I'm sure she is back in school. We both attend Georgetown."

"Okay, what time did you leave this party? Did you leave alone or with someone?"

"I left alone and I think it was 12:10. It wasn't long after the countdown I was starting to feel sick and just needed some fresh air."

"As you left did you notice anything suspicious?"

"Not really I was just walking and thinking and when I really got out of my head I noticed that I was lost and I was going to make my way back to the party."

"Why didn't you just call an Uber?"

"Well I didn't want to leave alone, I was going to go back home with a guy I noticed who was checking me out. But when I turned around, I kept hearing voices in the dark."

"Voices? What were they saying?"

"They kept saying I wasn't good enough, that I will forever be his, that I am not loved. Just very negative voices."

"How many voices do you think it was?"

"I don't know, maybe 3 or 4."

"What happened after that?"

"I don't know I got scared and I was starting to run but I slipped on some ice and I remember trying to crawl to a tree to get up but it all went black after that."

"Who is he?" Detective Garcia says, interrupting the flow of the interrogation.

"Excuse me?"

"You said that the voices said that 'you will forever be his.' So who is he?" Detective Garcia's suspicion is growing.

I pause trying to think hard about what I was going to say. Looking at the officers I could see that they wanted to label me as a crazy lady. "I am not sure, for all I know I could have been blacked out from being drunk, my dreams tend to be nightmarish and visual."

"Well your leg was broken in your dream, but also your leg was broken in real life, that is one vivid dream. Plus we saw the trail of blood from where you were crawling, but you rolled down a hill and fell into a hole. That is why you probably could no longer see the tree that was 5 feet away. I think you have a pretty good memory of your reality, not necessarily great relocation of your dreams.

"Well I was drunk officer, trying to get back to the hotel I was staying at."

"Hotel? Why wouldn't you live with your mom over here?"

"Well, we had an argument awhile back and I made the decision to not stay under her roof."

"When was this argument?"

"Christmas Eve, why is that relevant, Detective Garcia?"

"Just trying to get as much information as we can," Detective Roland buds in. "We don't think what happened to you was an accident, we are just trying to get to the bottom of who might have a motive to hurt you. Now if you don't mind answering the question, where were you on Christmas Eve?"

"There was a Christmas party at the Jones'."

"Now going back to Detective Garcia's question: What was the argument about?" Detective Garcia quiet in the back folding his arms. Intrigued and impatient waiting for something to slip up so he could condemn me.

"I think that is enough questions, officers." My mother steps in so I wouldn't need to feel ashamed for speaking on what happened."

"Okay, I get it. One more though. Where was the New Year's party located?"

"Umm, 6180 Tarrant Lane."

"Hmm, okay." The detectives get up and start to head for the door.

"Wait, detective. What was that hmm for?"

"Well where we discovered your blood and where Mr. Ethan claimed he found you, you were on Crowe's Drive. That is six miles away from where the party was.

Chapter TWELVE

"SIX MILES AWAY..." I kept tossing and turning, hearing these same words floating around in my head. Living rent free. How is this possible? What happened that night?

As the rest of the night became restless I couldn't help but think the following morning of what Dr. Arlo said. Of really trying to remember what happened to let the memory try and come back no matter how painful it is.

"Good Morning Paulina," Dr. Arlo says while coming into my room. "Today you finally get released back into the world, how are you feeling?"

"I am doing okay,"

"What's wrong Paulina?"

"Doctor, can I be honest with you?"

"Of course"

"Can I actually overcome this trauma?"

"Are you afraid that if you dive deeper into realizing the truth that it won't set you free? That instead it will drown you in fear, shame, and even torment?"

"Well, yes."

"Paulina, one thing I know is that when you stand in front of your giants and have faith more in the power of light, then know that darkness can not stay."

"What light"

"Hope," he said with such a compassionate look on his face. "That there can be good coming out of this situation."

"I guess, I don't know what goodness can come from here."

"Well start with this, how your story already brings hope and restoration. Look, you are completely healed from all your physical injuries, just a couple of bruises that will go away soon. And just some minor physical therapy to make sure everything is operating okay. Think of it like a tune up on a car. Or how about that you are alive after your wounds were exposed to cold weather."

"Thanks Doctor Arlo, I will take all that into consideration."

"You're welcome Paulina. I will have Nurse Johnson here to get all of these wires off of you and give you your release papers," he says with a confident smile.

"Thank you again."

He walks out and I am left once again to my thoughts and pondering on everything he had said.

"Hello Ms. Saville," a gentle sweet voice breaks me from my concentration. "I am here to remove your IV and heart monitor and I need your signature for this release form."

"Okay."

"Do we need to call you an Uber?"

"No need," hearing a familiar voice. I look over and see Ethan in the doorway swinging his keys around his finger smiling like he is ready to get me out of here."

"Mr. Arlo, so glad to see you. I know she will be in great hands," Nurse Johnson says while turning to me, giving me a wink. "Well after she changes she is all yours. So please come with me and we will leave her be while she gets ready."

"Yes ma'am," he says while giving her a chuckle and looking back at me before he closes the door."

As I am getting up out of the bed touching the floor I wondered if I should get my cane and walk to the bathroom or just walk on my own. I shook that thought away just as quickly as it entered and reached for my cane. I felt that I needed it for support. I went to the bathroom and started to get ready. I grab my stuff and open the door, mentally getting prepared to leave this room, this building, this place. I felt like I was leaving behind something that was fulfilling and satisfying; even purposeful. Not just that, but a place that made me feel so comfortable and welcomed no matter what. I wasn't ready to leave that behind. As I looked out into the hallway I saw Ethan looking up at me and smiling, he got up out of his chair and placed his hands in his pocket, waiting for me to make the first move. I step forward looking straight into his eyes and all I can feel is this passion and sense of security from him. Knowing inside that I can count on him to be here, to rely on him and that no matter what happens outside these walls he will always be right there. I go up to him and he extends his arm implying for me to grab it, as if he was confirming exactly what I was feeling. I grab his hand and hold it tight letting him know that I don't ever want to let it go. As we went outside and the sun began to shine on us, the fondness of being in the sun after being inside for so long still didn't compare to the warmth and sensitivity to Ethan's touch. His light causes even the sun to blush, no comparison because unlike the sun, Ethan's light doesn't hide behind the clouds.

"Here you are ma'am your chariot awaits"

"Haha, thank you my good sir." As I got into the car and he sealed me in, I knew at that moment I...

Ding, Ding

Cypher: Hello sexy, where have you been? I know you haven't forgotten about me already.

What does he want? I haven't heard from him since I sent him an email telling him I was stuck in the hospital and I needed to stay here for a while and he gave me more of a blow off. I just threw my phone to the ground. I had so much anger inside I felt that rage, betrayal, and a sharp pain started to arise within me. How dare he have the nerve to reach out to me after all this time, and make it about him.

"Paulina?"

"Yes."

"Are you okay, I've been talking to you, even calling your name."

Oh my goodness, I got so consumed in anger that I completely blocked out Ethan. "Yes, I am okay. Sorry I guess I was just lost in my thoughts."

"Penny for your thoughts?"

What would I tell him? Where do I even start? How would he feel about me afterwards? Would he leave me because I disgust him? I can't tell him anything about this. I know I should respond with something. "Well I guess I am just realizing how long it's been and how do I keep going after what seems like a lifetime?"

"Keep putting one foot forward, crawl forward, even roll forward. Either way you are headed in the right direction, no matter how big the step you take. Moving forward is moving forward, you can't go backwards that way."

"Never thought of it that way." I smile and look up at him and see him staring back at me matching my smile. I couldn't help but allow my cheeks to burn. As I was continuing to look out the window I couldn't help but embrace the scenery and the beauty of all that I missed and took advantage of by never acknowledging its existence.

Chapter THIRTEEN

"WELCOME HOME SWEETIE!" The first thing I heard as I got out of the car. My mom was running out of the house with her arms open wide, smiling from ear to ear. As I am making my way to my mother I embrace her in a hug. Tears came down my face, I felt like for a moment everything seemed perfect and right. My mother was really trying to be better, do better. Who knew that a traumatizing moment would bring us closer.

"Thank you mom, I really needed that."

"Well come in, we want to get you settled in, now I know you will only be here for a couple more weeks to finish up your sessions with Dr. Arlo, but I want to make you feel as comfortable as possible."

"Much appreciated."

"Now please get ready. I have some big news tonight to share with you, that is worth celebrating."

"But mom..."

"No, no, no don't but mom me. Off you go and meet me back down here in an hour young lady."

Good to know that some things haven't fully changed around here, I guess if it did then it would feel like there was a stranger living in this house. "Okay, I will go get ready."

"Thank you. Oh Ethan, please come here darling, I need you to take me somewhere real quick." Where could my mother possibly be going?

As I went into my room, everything looked exactly the same. The way I had left it, the interesting part of seeing that was even though my room hadn't changed I felt like I had. As I got out of the shower I went to my closet trying to figure out what to wear for this special occasion. Who knows for what. I couldn't find anything that fit right, that felt like me. I started to get frustrated, mainly because who was I any more. Something seemed different, even uncomfortable. There was no longer a shell over me. With everything that has happened in just a few months, there was this shadow of shame and guilt forecasting over me, like I actually deserved what happened to me. I started to feel my chest tighten, my breathing seemed to get shorter, and the room was shaking. I collapse to the ground, my palms sweating, what is happening. I started to scream and cry at the same time. "Go away! Go away! Please go away!"

"Paulina!" Ethan comes running into the room. He gets down on the floor and grabs me, wrapping his arms around me, I fall into them. He held me so close and tight that I felt the tension starting to disappear, like it had no more power. Ethan's presence alone was my safe haven. Then he whispers into my ear, "I will never let you go my love."

We stayed on the ground for what seemed like a lifetime. When I am with him everything is peaceful and calm, can I stay right here forever with him? I moved away, staring at him, thanking him without any words. He grabs my neck and slowly starts to pull me in closer and gives me a kiss on my forehead. I sigh in relief. He then gets up and extends out his hand to me to help me up. I grabbed it and he pulled me in closer. My heart was racing in excitement of what could possibly be the next move. Will I be able to be ready for this? A million thoughts came into my head, a million different scenarios played out. And yet not any of them was called into play. He starts to dance with me. What is going on? He started to smile as he knew I was tense. That same smile gave me ease. We are laughing as he is twirling me slowly in my bath towel, making sure I am not putting too much pressure on my foot. "You are something else, you know that."

He pulls me in closer, one hand on my hip the other in my hand, "Nothing else in this whole world compares to how you are something much more." My eyes lit up, filled with such awe. I felt like I was in a cartoon where the character sees the one they love and their eyes pop out with hearts. He couldn't help but smile, knowing what I was saying through my eyes. This quiet conversation spoke more words and was louder than any other conversation that would ever take place again. "Here I have something for you."

"How do you always have something for me?" He just laughs at me and pulls out a black bag, big enough to hold a dress. He unzips the bag and pulls out this most stunning emerald green dress. A one shoulder that connects with an emerald green flower, it expands into a flowy dress, a pattern of two different greens at the bottom. This dress was perfect, absolutely beautiful. "Oh my goodness! This dress is incredible. Thank you so much, you didn't have to do this."

"I thought you may have needed something different and new." I smile at him. "I need to go pick up Mrs. Saville, we will be back in 20 minutes to come get you."

"Okay, I'll be ready by then, thank you." As he turned around to close the door I couldn't help but want him to stay, stay with me forever.

"Oh, my lovely Paulina, you look amazing. What a gown," my mother says as I make my way down the stairs.

"Thank you mother."

"Okay we need to get going, we have to get to the restaurant we have reservations."

"Okay." I really wanted to say, of course we do. But I decided against that. If my mother is trying, then the least I can do is the same thing. My mother's phone had dropped and I reached down to pick it up, "Oh no honey I got it." As she got it, her jacket lifted up a bit and I saw what seemed like teeth marks on her wrist. The moment I noticed that I started to get a weird taste in my mouth. Stuck in my place, as if I was paralyzed I had a flashback of that night and could see five figures hovering over me, talking, pinning me down, I tried to escape and...

"Paulina, come on darling." I shook off the memory and started to head to the car and get in. As we were driving along the road I glanced over at my mom a few times and noticed that she was smiling a lot while texting. I couldn't help but think about what I remembered seeing and what was that bite mark on my mother? I turned to look out the window in hopes that it would turn those thoughts off. Why does this road look so familiar, where is she taking me? When we took that final turn I knew it,

"Cerchio! Why are you bringing me back here?"

"Honey I know what it seems, but please remain calm this will all make sense I promise."

"How could this possibly make sense, this is Mr. Eric Jones' restaurant that he brought us to before the Christmas party."

"I know what it seems like, please just trust me." Before I could speak Ethan is opening up my door extending out his hand for me to grab. I take a deep breath and grab it. Completely on guard the moment my feet touch the ground. Ready for any chaotic battle that awaited behind the restaurant doors. Ready to defend myself.

"Welcome Mrs. Eva Saville and Ms. Paulina Saville, please follow me to your table."

Taking a deep breath with every step, super anxious to face the Jones'.

"Eva and Paulina! Welcome!" Mrs. Jones comes rushing up to us giving us a hug. "Please sit down."

"Where is Mr. Jones this evening, will he not be joining us?"

"Well Paulina, because of you opening up my eyes to many things, Eric and I got a divorce and this restaurant among other things is mine." Wow, did I really cause a marriage to break? Did I cause so much chaos that I ruined something that is supposed to be sacred because of my own mess. How could I? "I know you are probably thinking the worst right now about yourself, I can see the panic on your face. Trust me Paulina, this was long overdue, we both were unfaithful and had our own unresolved issues. This should have taken place years ago. I am not angry with you, I am actually thankful and grateful for you. So please don't give yourself so much credit."

I swallowed those words as if it was a horse pill. I quickly grabbed my glass of water to wash it down. As I was sitting there staring at my consequences in the face, I couldn't help but still take the blame, just because someone says it is not your fault doesn't erase the complete feeling that somehow it is. If it wasn't for Mrs. Jones catching Mr. Jones and I this wouldn't have happened. "Will you excuse me for a second?" I got up as quickly as I could and headed to the bathroom, crying at the sink.

"Paulina?" A soft quiet voice calling through the locked door.

"Ethan?" I open up the door swiftly, "What are you doing?"

"Well I was just leaving the men's room and I saw you crying all the way here. I think you left a trail, you may need to get the 'Wet Floor' sign." Ethan made an attempt to make me laugh, he noticed that his joke had not made me crack a smile so he continued, "Why are you drowning in a pool of your own tears?"

"I am the reason Mr. and Mrs. Jones' got a divorce." I lean into Ethan crying, just wanting him to hold me as I tried to cry every last piece of sadness and regret. How it burned, it seemed like every tear came with a sharp stabbing pain in my chest being removed and being placed back in at the same time.

"Paulina?" He pushes me slightly so he can look at me, my head still down, he gently grabs my chin to lift my gaze up, "look at me please." I eventually look up at him and he is staring into my eyes, taking his time before he responds, observing me. The way he was looking at me made me curious and intrigued as to what he was going to say. "Don't give yourself so much credit, stop playing into the hands of being a victim. Yes, you did what you did and that action can't be taken back. There is a thing called giving yourself grace and forgiving yourself. Learn from what took place and try to not do it again. Not saying that situation or feelings won't arise again, just remember this moment of how it makes you feel and how you don't want to experience this ever again. You helped open Mrs. Jones' eyes to something she herself has been trying to hide away from, and since it was forced to be brought forth into the light she had to face a decision she chose to make. She chose to either stay with him or leave him, and isn't it better for her to go and live a fulfilling life free from a man who stopped being faithful to her because he was consumed by his own selfish desires? Even vice versa."

"Playing a victim?!" I quickly got myself out of his hands. "How dare you accuse me of being a victim to something so traumatizing. Please go away and leave me alone." Expeditiously I walked away, not even looking back. I found my way back to the table where my mom and Patricia were drinking and laughing the night away.

"Paulina! Please come sit, is everything okay sweetie? You have a little bit of mascara running." I wiped my face feeling embarrassed. "I have some big news that I have been dying to share with you. After the Christmas party me and Patricia hadn't spoken for a few days. She reached out to me apologizing for the way she reacted towards me..."

"Yes, I was completely out of line for assuming the worst." She looks at my mother grabbing her hand providing sweet comfort and assuring her words were sealed forever.

"Well, as we sat down and discussed everything, she told me how so many people from the party truly enjoyed the event I put on. She gave me a list of new clients and I just signed off on an office space. I have my own party planning business!"

"Wow! Mom that is incredible, I am super happy for you. I really am proud of you."

"Thank you sweetie," happy tears seem to stream down her face, more beautiful than a waterfall. I reached out and cherished my mother. No matter how upset I was with Ethan, it was not going to stop me from congratulating and celebrating my mother. I know she worked hard for that party. I never really saw my mom more motivated and passionate. "That is why I was also in Costa Rica, it was a vacation and also a business trip talking to a new client."

"I totally get it mom, it is okay."

"Paulina, how are you holding up after your accident and all? I am glad you are doing better and not really needing your cane as much this evening." My cane?

I totally forgot that I even had it. Didn't I just run to the bathroom? Didn't I run away from Ethan? "Paulina?"

"Oh, sorry I was, nevermind. Yes I am doing better. Dr. Arlo is amazing. Him and his team took really good care of me."

"Well I am glad to see you doing better. And up on your feet." She smiled raising her glass, her sleeve raised up and all I could see was a mark similar to my mothers.

Chapter FOURTEEN

"WELL, I WILL be back for spring break."

"That is so far away though."

"Mom, it is literally like six weeks away."

"I know, everything that has been going on I..." she starts to cry. I grabbed her, assuring her that everything was going to be okay.

"Okay, mom I need to go before I miss my flight."

"Yes, yes. I get it. Ugh, I know, I know. Why did you get an Uber though? You know Ethan would have taken you."

"Yeah, well I didn't want him to go out of his way, I am sure you are busy with your own thing today."

"Yeah, uh huh sure. I don't know what is going on with you two. I do know as much, that man loves you and would do anything for you. Stop running away from him."

"What, ha, I, I don't know what crazy nonsense you are talking about. There is nothing..."

"Yeah sure sweetie. I love you, now go. I'll talk to you later." She gave me a kiss on my cheek.

Ethan: I know you didn't want to see me, I will always be here no matter what.

Me: Thanks Ethan.

Being on the plane brought back that crazy dream the last time. Other memories filled my mind like Deni, Cypher, and Georgetown. I felt like there was no escaping my reality. I just keep going back and forth from one traumatizing pain to another. This cycle doesn't ever seem to cease. All I want is to break free, but how? Finally touching down in Arlington I get mentally prepared to take on my next battle. That is to finally see Deni.

Chapter FOURTEEN

"Lina! Welcome home! I was wondering when you would be back."

"Can it Deni, I haven't heard from you since New Years, I just came here to get my stuff. I am going to live somewhere else. What a best friend you are."

"Lina, don't be like that. Come on, I think you are overreacting here. You know how crazy school gets around here. I needed to keep up on my school work. I am sorry I didn't reach out enough while you were in the 'hospital' but come on, you had that sexy man candy by your side. I know it."

"Stop it! Don't talk about him like that. I was in the hospital and really, school work? With all the empty bottles lying around. Plus you didn't even reach out once. Look I didn't come here to argue with you, I came here to get my stuff. Find yourself another roommate."

"Haha, Oh I have. In fact I found two." Coming from out of the corner was none other than...

"Zared? Ansa?"

"Well, well, well, look who has decided to finally grace us with her presence."

"Yeah, we began to worry about you, you know it is not much of a party without you here," Zared leans up on the couch giving me a wink.

"Really Zared!" Deni kicks his feet.

"What babe? I was just saying. I know she missed partying with us, among other things."

"Whatever Zared. I need to go. You guys have fun living out your life. I want no part of it."

"Okay," Ansa gets up twirling her hair coming towards me. "That is what you say now, you will come back when you get bored. And we will be right here."

"We will?" Deni asks with such confusion.

"Of course, Deni. That's what friends are for right?"

"Oh, yeah; right." They all just smile at me.

"No thank you, now if you can please move out of my way that would be great."

"As you wish."

Finally, I can breathe. I am living on campus in my own dorm. Probably something I should have done a long time ago. The thing is though I didn't even think my supposed best friend would treat me like this. Whatever, I am going to shake all of this off. I will go and run a bath. I am thankful that my mom set all of this up for me. What a beautiful view of the campus. This is probably better so I don't get distracted by all the parties and craziness. I start to drench my stress in the bathtub in hopes that the bubbles relax every tight muscle. Cucumbers on my eyes and music playing in my ears.

Ring, Ring

The moment I actually get to relax and get in tune with the tunes, gets interrupted; go figure. I answered the call, "Hello?"

"Well hello sexy, I saw you back on campus today. I am guessing I will get to see you tomorrow in class. After class would work just fine too."

"Cypher?!"

"Well yeah, who else would it be calling you and wanting to see you."

"Oh now you want to see me, now you care to know how I am doing."

"I care enough to help ease your tension. I'm sure the past few weeks have been rough on you. Come on, let me help you now. You know I had to be here and teach a class and grade papers. Can I get a pass?"

"Goodnight Cypher, now leave me alone."

"Awe C'mon, just remember all the good times we had, how many times you got to say my name among other things."

"No."

"I prefer to hear the sound of you saying '*yes*'." Ugh, why can this man be such a jerk and yet so irresistible, knowing how to get me started. The way he charms me. How could I forget all the wonderful times we had, in every position, every touch. No, I can't give in. "I know you are thinking about everything, I can hear your heavy breathing and slight moan through the phone. Tell me how wet you are?"

"I'm in the bathtub so clearly I am drenched."

"Ooo, even better. Imagine that I am there in the tub with you. And you and I play a game of how long I can hold my breath."

Ding, Ding

I get a notification and I can't help but move my phone from my face to see what it was and of course it was;

Ethan: Goodnight Paulina, may your night be as sweet as all of the fine chocolate in the world. No matter how rich it is, it doesn't compare to how rich your heart is.

Of course I would see that right now just when I am about to have phone sex with Cypher.

"Lina? Are you still there?"

"I have to go, Cypher. I am not in the mood right now."

Click

Even though I was angry with Ethan, I couldn't help but think about the other stuff he said. That it made sense, as per usual. Either way, I know that it completely killed the mood. I am not sure how I entirely feel about that. I am stuck in between two different worlds. Wanting both, but knowing that I can only be loyal to one. Cypher and Ethan both bring two different things to the table. Only one can feed me food that will help grow me and the other will slowly poison me.

Beep, Beep

Ugh, please five more minutes.

Beep, Beep

Fine, fine! I am getting up. Stop yelling at me. How can a little phone command so much from me? Doesn't even talk. "People talk through you, you know."

"I'm sorry, what was that Paulina?"

"Oh nothing Siri, my apologies."

"No worries."

I forgot Siri does live in that, doesn't she. I guess she has every right to command someone else, since she gets commanded all day. What am I doing? I need to get ready for class. Not for me thinking about Siri.

"Welcome back Ms. Paulina. I see that we are running a bit late this morning. I guess your extended break made you forget how to be on time."

"I am sorry Professor Dana. It will not happen again."

"Good, it better not. Now class let's talk about art in various cultures. Chris please depict your theory about Rome." I shuffle through the seats to sit down. Completely flustered. How could I be late on my first day back. It felt good to be back here. Just trying to focus on the goal at hand. Not focusing on everything that had happened. Class seemed to roll on just like any other time. I also have never been more ready and prepared for this class. But we know all things have to end at some point, except for eternity. Just the thought of it scared me a bit. How we get used to everything ending all around us, until eternity plays its part. How can anyone fathom that? As class had ended Professor Dana called out to me,"Ms. Paulina, please come see me." I headed over to her desk, interested to know what was on her mind. "How are you holding up?"

"I am doing okay, just trying to put one foot in front of the other."

"Good to hear, may I ask what happened? Your email just said you were in an accident and that you would be out for a while. Thank you for keeping up with the lectures and thank you for emailing me your release form from your doctor. That is quite mature of you."

"You're welcome," I said, pretty impressed with myself.

"Well I am curious as to why you were late this morning," she says, ripping the smile off of my face.

"I know I am so sorry, I just overslept. I guess I was just adjusting to being back here. And the cops ruled it out as an animal attack. My leg probably got rebroken by the animal stepping on me or something. I really don't remember much from that night."

"Well do you believe that is what happened?"

"Uh, yeah. Of course. I do live in Colorado near the mountains, it is quite possible."

"Your answer doesn't seem too confident and is filled with many filler words, hiding a certain denial. Have you actually tried to remember what happened or do you keep burying it down because you don't want to face the reality of what actually happened. Anyone can focus on a possible outcome and yet never can live in it because it is not actually the truth. Something to think about while you write your end of the year paper that is due, very soon."

"Yes ma'am, thank you." I turned around and walked away, slumping my shoulders. Maybe, just maybe Professor Dana has a point. And because of that why does that scare me enough to seek out the truth.

Chapter FIFTEEN

"OKAY, PAULINA. YOU got this, you can do this. This isn't something too hard or difficult for you to do. Don't let this thing beat you. Just breathe!"

"It's not rocket science!" Dillon shouts. I let the ball go.

"Oh there it goes, you got this! Strike! You go Paulina. I knew I picked the right person for the team."

"Haha, thank you Rebecca. I really needed this. Thank you guys for getting me out tonight. I know I haven't been really close to you and Dillon so..."

"All good Paulina. We totally get it," Dillon says with a calm smile tucking his hands into his pocket. "How are you doing, I know you have been here for a couple weeks now, you seem like you are doing quite well in Professor Cypher's class. How did you manage to do that?"

"Well, I guess right now I am just ignoring him. Not paying attention to him in a way that could potentially distract me. Let me tell you it isn't easy that is for sure. Do you know what the final assignment will be this year?"

"All I know is that he takes the words we say very seriously."

"Wait, Rebecca; you are telling me that it is a presentation. It is not a written essay we give to him to read?"

"No way, he makes us get up and talk about what this class has done for us and why we would recommend it to others coming in."

"How can you fail based on an opinionated response? That makes no sense."

"Professor Cypher's grading techniques make no sense to us either. That is why we need your help Paulina. How can we pass?"

"How would I know, I can't seem to do anything right."

"No, there is something about you, I know it, she knows it. You are a researcher, you search for facts and clarity. Please help bring clarity to us. I can't fail another year or else I will be trapped in this cycle forever, a never ending torture. Failure will torment me day and night; eventually believing there is no hope to come and save me. Doesn't it scare you that history is becoming your present and being your forever future, that time doesn't change?"

History, cycle, no hope, I couldn't help but to think of Professor Dana's last writing assignment and how this somehow ties into what is going on now. When she gave this assignment months ago I didn't think this was anything relevant for today. But oddly enough it seemed to have aligned with this perfect timing and moment. 'Being trapped in this circle forever?' In this circle? *In Questo Cerchio*? Cerchio, Mrs. Jones restaurant, Mrs Jones and my mother having a similar mark. That taste in my mouth comes back, oh no. My mind gets rushed back to the night of the accident, I got sucked in like a black hole. I started to see me on the ground in the street, panicked and crying out. Looking behind me, trying to get to the tree. I see five shadows rushing by, one of them takes my broken leg and as they were pulling it, they snapped it back into place. The look on their face seemed to be shocked as if that was not meant to happen. As I am crying another one turns me on my back and places their hand over my lips, to keep me from screaming. I take my hand and grab their wrist. As I used all my strength to remove their hand I also leaned in to bite their wrist. As they scream in horror someone else comes up and starts hitting me with a rock on my eye, causing me to let go and I get pushed to fall into the pit...

"Paulina! Are you okay?" Next thing I knew I was on the ground, hyperventilating. Grabbing on to my chest.

"Please, make this thought go away, I don't want to go back to that."

"Okay, okay." Rebecca and Dillon get on the floor and start to surround me, hugging me. "It's going to be okay. That thing doesn't have to haunt you anymore." Even though her words held some truth to it, it lacked an answer to the **how** part. I guess that is where I needed to go and search to find that answer. But tonight was not that night either.

"Thank you guys for walking me back to my room. I really appreciate it."

"Of course, we just wanted to make sure you got back here safely."

I gave a light smile. "Goodnight guys, I will see you tomorrow."

"Goodnight Paulina, get some rest." Dillon said with a sense of worry in his voice. I shut the door and started to slip into my pajamas. I lay in bed not trying to focus on what just happened at the bowling alley. I need to get my mind off everything. I will try to watch tv and go to bed, what else could I do?

Cypher: Hey you, do you want some company?"

Me: Sure, come over. I'll send you the dorm room number.

I begin to take a quick shower and put on something that would be more memorable.

Knock, Knock

"Come in, the door is unlocked." Cypher opens up the door wearing an all black button down shirt, black slacks and black shoes. Standing in the doorway he can't help but look at me up and down as I am on my bed on my knees, in a cute red lace corset lingerie. My hair down and wavy giving him that look to come have his way with me, there would be no safe word tonight. As he is intrigued, undressing me with his eyes and waits to make every dirty thought be made known, just like words coming off the page creating the exact image right in front of you. Fantasy is finally becoming a reality.

Cypher walks towards me and as he hovers over me he stares me down, he grabs me by the neck and starts to kiss me, his other hand is on my lower back pushing me to lay on my back. Those sweet and fire burning kisses start to make their tracks to my neck, then down to my chest. Taking his leg he starts to spread mine, each nibble becomes more and more intense. Causing me to scratch his back with the same intensity.

"I want to feel every nail digging into my back," he says this while removing his shirt one button at a time. It felt like he was taking forever that I was starting to get impatient. As he saw me squirming to try to get up to help him, he squeezed his thighs onto my thighs keeping me trapped. "No, you can wait, just like you made me wait." I lay back in complete frustration. Then he finally removes his shirt, and then his belt. As he was leaning in I could feel how much he wanted to play. Grabbing my hands and placing them over my head; he said, "You are mine, tell me I'm yours and you can have all of me."

"Your mine, it's all yours," I say as I moan that out loud. The moment I said it he began to enter into me, each thrust having its own uniqueness, some softer than others. "Oh, Cypher. Please keep going..."

"We interrupt this program to bring you some news..."

"What did you say Cypher?"

"According to the new rules here at Georgetown..."

"Excuse me," I wake up and I see my tv is still playing. Wow, that was a very vivid dream. Wait a minute. I look down using one of my hands to lift up the covers. I couldn't help but see how my dreams kind of made their way out. Pleasing myself, that is definitely new. Well, I might as well finish now.

"Good morning class, Spring Break is around the corner. Now I don't want to put pressure on you; well who am I kidding, I wouldn't be me if I didn't cause you to sweat." Cypher starts to have that chuckle and looks right at me. Everyone else starts to laugh. "On a serious note your end of the year presentation is due the week after your Spring Break. I have the schedule of who is going to present on what day. So before you leave today, come check it out, because this is your only chance to see this schedule. It will go away."

"Wow, harsh much?"

"Excuse me Lina, did you have something to say?"

Oops, that was not supposed to be heard. "Uh, no Professor Cypher. Nothing at all."

"No, please come flatter us with what you want to say."

"Uh..."

"Uh, what? Don't keep us waiting."

Come on, you can do this. I took a deep breath, "Don't you think that is harsh, why do we only get one chance to see this schedule? What does that accomplish?"

"It accomplishes the fact that in this life you only get one chance to make it right, there are no other opportunities that are the same. Maybe this will help you all to be responsible for your own actions. You know what, class is dismissed. You all now have one minute to come up here and see what the presentation schedule is, thanks to Miss Lina. Starting now." Everyone sighs in anger and rushes up to the front. Cypher sits back on his desk, crossing his arms staring at me. Finding pleasure in hearing the ruffle paper, and fast heart beats. I finally squeezed my way down there to find out what day I needed to present. "Times up. Looks like Paulina, you are the only one who didn't get to see what day you presented. Now you have to guess what day that is. Hmm, don't get it wrong, because you only get one chance." I hear Ansa and Zared laughing in the back as they are walking out of class, Deni follows right behind them looking at me with some concern.

"That is not fair Professor."

"Life isn't fair, and yet we just have to deal with it."

"Why are you doing this?"

"Lina, you are free to leave now, I have nothing more to say to you."

"Free? What do you think, you own me?" Cypher begins to clinch his cheeks hand rolling it into a fist. Next thing I knew I was walking away from him and he grabs my arm and spins me around leaning me up to his filing cabinet. "What?" I was completely terrified of what he would do next.

"I will own you, once you say those words that I know you have been dying to tell me. There is no one else I want to be here by my side forever. Just finally let your heart decide that you want me, and only me." Grabbing the back of my neck he pulls me in to give me a hard kiss. Filled with the desire that I know I missed and longed for. Someone who wants me, makes me feel like they need me forever. I kiss him back just as harshly, biting his lower lip. Tugging his shirt to tell him to

233

take it off. Grabbing my waist and lifting me up he takes me to the desk. How I missed him.

After that morning, I needed to take a trip down to the cafe. I could really use a coffee and a muffin to recharge. I walked into the cafe and I noticed Ansa, Zared, and Deni sitting at our table, just looking at me. Ansa waves to me, I give a slight wave back. I hop in the line waiting to place my order.

Ding, Ding

Ansa: Come sit with us when you are done.

I look up and see her waiving me over. I give her a thumbs up.

Ding, Ding

Cypher: That was amazing, worth the wait. The way you get me going in a way only you can.

I couldn't help but smile from ear to ear, I sent him a blushing smiley face and blew him a kiss.

Ding, Ding

Ethan: I saw this and thought of you. It was a picture of two deers, one a doe and the other a buck embracing each other, with three fawns playing around them.

Ethan: It reminded me of how you told me that when you were a kid you saw something similar to this and you knew there was such a thing as a perfect family somewhere.

Wow I can't believe he remembered that. That was a very special moment in my life. As if it was a kiss from heaven, a spring of hope. I saw this not long after my father died and my mom was in and out of relationships. This was truly thoughtful. I saved the picture and made it as my screensaver.

Me: Thank you Ethan, I can't believe you remembered. That is super sweet and thoughtful of you. :)

"Lina, your order is up." I swiftly looked up, and I cracked my neck.

"Ow, thank you so much. I guess I needed that too."

"I get it, if we can't afford a masseuse might as well get it somewhere else."

"Ha, yeah I guess you are right. Wait? I haven't ordered yet."

"Oh, your friends over there said you might be coming and ordered ahead for you. When they gave the signal of waving their hand towards you, that was also for us to make your order, a blueberry muffin and an Iced Caramel Mocha Latte, correct?"

"Uh, yes that is correct. Okay, well what do I owe you then?"

"Nothing ma'am, it is also paid for by your friends."

"Okay, um thank you."

I make my way over to them. "Why did you do that?"

"Why wouldn't we? You may not talk to us, but we never said we would stop being your friends."

"Friends know how to be there for one another, not abandon them by not hearing a single word from them when they go through something traumatizing."

"Oh, don't think you are better than us. We all go through our own traumatizing stuff. You don't see us moping around, we just get through it, not waiting for someone to come hold us all the way to being healed. Once, did you decide to step out of your own little bubble and think that maybe I was going through something, and I didn't have the strength to reach out to you. Being consumed by my own pit of disaster, how could I be there for you?"

"Oh Deni, I am sorry I didn't know. Please forgive me. You are right, I have been so caught up in my own mess that

I totally forgot about you. Forgetting that you can have your own crap to deal with."

"Just remember that it is not all about you, and we are good." She gives me a smile saying that we are cool.

"So are you going to stand there, or you gonna pull up a chair?"

"Oh, only you Zared. I will sit for a while. We can catch up."

"That's my girl. We are glad to have you back."

We sat there laughing and catching up with what was going on. I missed this, having friendships. Feeling like I belong somewhere.

"So, do you remember anything from that night?"

"Zared, that is so impolite."

"I am just curious."

"It's okay Ansa, um I don't really remember much. There are some things I remember, but it is too painful to go back to that memory. I'd rather forget." They all look at eachother with smiles on their faces. "What?"

"Well we know the best way to forget about a traumatic experience and to get you back to your old self. Numbing everything so you don't have to think about it ever again."

"What is it? Don't keep me guessing. I'll do anything, to be free from this."

"Anything?" Deni said. As soon as she said that I felt my stomach tighten, what did I just agree to?

"Party!" They all scream together.

"Come out with us. There is a big party happening at The Ultimate Underground tonight. Come check it out with us. We will drink booze until we can't think any more. What do you say?"

I look at all of them, thinking. I did this before and yes for a moment it helped, but at some point it left me empty. If this is all that is offered in this world to heal me then why not. I guess there is nothing else out there. "Fine! Haha, let's go party it up."

"Yes! Woo! This is going to be amazing, meet us at the apartment at 10 then we will head out together sound good?"

"Okay, I will see you guys then. I have to go to my other class now, I don't want to be late."

"See you later."

As I walk away from them I see Dillon and Rebecca sitting at another table looking at me with complete concern. Slowly feeling their last and final hope was about to be gone. That their final chance at redemption was now in the rearview mirror. Complete sorrow was leaving my eyes. Because deep down I knew something wasn't right but I am not a superhero. How can I help anyone if I can't even help myself?

Chapter SIXTEEN

"SHE DOESN'T EVEN know what really happened to her."

"Yeah boss, the more and more we keep distracting her she won't ever want to find out."

"What about that other guy? Back in Colorado?"

"Trust me boss, she hasn't spoken to him in three weeks."

"She is mine, the more and more we keep her coming this way and she finally seals her fate with us with those final words we have won."

"Haha, yes boss. It will truly be another trophy added to your collection."

"Now go, torment her. Just long enough to keep her away from the truth. Bring her to me."

———————

"Lina, what did you get on your midterm?" Deni comes running up behind me.

"Hey Deni, I passed all my quizzes. I can't wait to show my mom," I said excitedly as I turned to face Deni.

"Oh are you going to facetime her right now? I don't mind telling her hi."

"Haha, no silly. I am going back to Colorado for Spring Break. I will tell her then."

"What?! You are going back to Colorado?" Deni said while having fear in her eyes, completely surprised and unaware of my answer.

"Yeah, of course," looking at her confused as to why she seems so disturbed. "Plus Doctor Arlo wanted me to have a check up appointment with him." I turn away to start walking towards my dorm.

"Oh, uh okay. Sorry I didn't realize that you were heading back to Colorado for the week." I could see Deni biting her nails uncontrollably.

"Deni wh..."

"Hey, what's happening for a week?" Zared comes up wrapping his arms around both of us.

"Lina here, is going back to Colorado for Spring Break," Deni says while crossing her arms and rolling her eyes.

"Why do you want to do that? Come to Mexico with us. Partying, bar hopping, plus the pleasure of meeting new people. We know how much you like that Lina." Ansa says while pulling my arm to bring me closer to her.

"I would, but my ticket is already paid for; I have to see my Doctor for a check up."

"Why? What is he going to say that we don't already know? You can walk, you are healed, go live your life. That is exactly why you need to come with us," Ansa proceeds to persist.

"Maybe another time, I really want to see my mom anyways. She and I rekindled our relationship and I know she has planned a big event that week and

I would love to support her. So far she is doing really well."

"Blah, blah, blah. Come on, yeah good for you and your mom's relationship, but you know there is no possible way that you will have a lot of fun there."

"Why not, because I am not out drinking and partying everyday? Maybe there is more to life than all of this. I have been numbing my feelings day in and day out. When it wears off it all comes rushing back." I am no longer drowning out the trauma with alcohol, because all the alcohol and the trauma is drowning me.

"Dang, chill. We get it. Fine, go to Colorado. We are going to have fun some-where else, not judging anyone and their decisions." I just roll my eyes and shake my head. They are not going to guilt trip me into going. I should have just gone back to my dorm instead they persuaded me to head back to Deni's apartment with them. I couldn't help but look over and see Deni give Ansa this look, which made very suspicious and uncomfortable. I thought that was very odd, but oh well. A part of me wanted to go back to Colorado and another part of me wanted to run away from there. I didn't want to see Doctor Arlo, he reminds me that my accident was real and Ethan reminds me of how I am not good enough to belong with a great guy like him. We get to Deni's apartment and Ansa waves over to me; "Lina, come here, try on this skirt and shirt I think it would look super cute on you."

"Okay, I am coming." I go into the bathroom and slip on the outfit she handed me. I look over in the body mirror hanging up behind the bathroom door. I think I look pretty good in this outfit, my legs are nicely tan. It is fitting quite well, really complimenting my figure. Mirror, mirror on the wall who looks fabulous above all, haha. Being your own encourager is self love at its finest.

"Don't keep us waiting queen, come out. We want to see how you look."

Alright here we go. "Ta-da! How fabulous do I look, I know I am killing it in this outfit."

"Uhh, no," Deni says, looking horrified.

"Yeah girl that outfit is not hitting. That skirt is way too low that your thigh fat is still jiggling and you aren't even moving." Ansa says in a snarky remark.

"Excuse me?!"

"That is definitely not doing your figure justice, I don't even mean that in a compliment way."

"Ansa! Why are you saying these things?"

"As your friend I am not going to let you go out here not looking your 100. Don't get crazy on me." Tears started to weld up in my eyes, what is she doing? "Look if you don't believe me we will get Zared in here, and you can get a man's perspective, okay. Oh Zared!"

"Yes?"

"Can you come here please, we need your honest opinion."

"Ugh, fine. I was only trying to pre-game over here you know." Zared walked in, with a shot in one hand and a mixed drink in the other. "What's up?"

"Tell me, would you even touch Lina in this outfit?"

Looking me up and down, my stance slumped, my left hand grabbing my right arm showing that I am not that confident. Afraid of what his response was going to be. I hear his laughter echoing in my head and says, "Not a chance. Sorry honey, look at your shoulders they make you look like you can be a linebacker. Wait, let me see if this helps." Taking back his shot and chugging his mix drink he comes back up for some air. "Wow, what a rush, okay let me look again," analyzing me one more time, "yeah, nope that didn't help, good luck getting any guy to look your way." Standing there with my jaw dropping he walks away without any remorse.

"See honey, I told you. That outfit was not your look. Here go change into something that is more conservative since you don't know how to have fun any more."

"What is your problem, why do you keep pressuring me into going to Mexico with you guys? I can do whatever I want for my Spring Break."

Ansa gets up off of the bed and stares me down, pressing herself against me. "You're not worth the pressure sweetie. You are nothing without any of us, so don't kid yourself. Now you are either with us or you're not, who cares about going back to Colorado there is nothing there for you, we are the ones who truly care for you. Do you really buy the fact that your mom couldn't reach any service for three weeks, please I'm sure she could have come back at any time, she was probably too busy sitting on another man's lap, ha who knows maybe more than just one."

Ansa's words were cutting me, everything that I had questioned in my mind I could hear out loud. Why did I feel like she knew me better than I knew myself? What if she is right, maybe I should just go to Mexico. Who cares about what is in Colorado, I don't need reminders there, I can go somewhere that is new and different, where no one knows me or what I have done and been through. I straighten myself up, "What the heck, let's go partying and in one week let's go to Mexico!"

"That's my girl, here is a shot for you. And here is this outfit that I bought just for you. Go take a shower and get ready, we leave in an hour."

I see nothing but strobe lights bouncing off of every wall and everyone. Loud techno music blasting through every cup. The way this place was bumping it would make Berlin's nightclubs seem like it was amateur hour there. The room is spinning and I am just dancing on every guy who decided to come press themselves against me. At some point I was overheating so I grabbed Deni and we headed towards the bar. We get another drink to help cool us down just laughing and having a good time. "Can we please get two dirty martinis, and make them filthy."

"Of course ma'am, only the best for you," the bartender gives me a wink.

"Ooo, Lina, that man is flirting big time, are you going to get at that."

"I'm way ahead of you Deni, he will know my name by the end of the night, he will be saying it non stop. Nearly begging me not to stop."

"Here you are ladies, and for you ma'am this is completely defiled."

"I like the sound of that."

"I much rather like the sound of your moans in my ear."

"Oh, yes! Keep going! Don't stop!"

In the back of the alley the bartender and I are going at it. In the moment full of passion yet still empty. Neither of our hearts were in it, our motivation was booze and lust. Physically it felt amazing, the way we were moving together. How could something so lifeless be so phenomenal. This man knew what he was doing. As we finish he sets me down.

"Wow, you are incredible. I never met someone who can do such tricks down there." Buckling up his belt and zipping up his pants, he continues to say, "I wanna see you again. Next weekend sounds good?"

"I'll be in Mexico then," I grab his shirt to pull him closer and kiss him, "the weekend after can be a different story if you are willing to wait that long for me."

"You know it Lina, I'll be right here waiting for you. Goodnight."

"Goodnight Chris"

I start walking back to the campus. It is about three in the morning. Maybe I should head over to Deni's place, I still have the key. It seemed a lot closer. As I was walking this dark and lonely street, the street lights began to become hazy. Even being blocks away from the club the atmosphere was still causing this place to not stop spinning. Searching for my phone in my bag, all my stuff comes out.

"Oh great!" I get on the ground to pick up my stuff and as I look at my phone, it is completely dead. "Go figure." I put it in my bag and I looked back up where I saw a street light out into the distance, it started to flicker. I tilt my head, curious as to why it was all of a sudden flickering. As it was flickering there was something in the far off distance I saw a tree. There was a light switch going off in my head, the light post was turning into a tree, but not just any tree. The tree that was in Colorado. I started to fill a cold rush going down my spine, goosebumps going up my arms. And I began to hear laughter out in the distance. Panic started to become like an old friend. I turn around and see five shadows reaching out to me, mocking me. I get up and start running. Trying to get away, I slip and fall. "Oh no, not again." The darkness kept coming closer. I can feel them trying to take my last breath knocking me over by hitting me with a rock. I ended up falling into a pit, my leg was stuck between two rocks.

As I tried to take it out I twisted my leg wrong, breaking that leg again.

"You are mine, you have made your choice, and that is good enough for me. Now come join me for all eternity." A dark and disturbed voice with red eyes starts gnashing his teeth, who happened to be Cypher. The other four shadows approached me and as they did I began to see their faces. I couldn't believe who I saw; my mother, Deni, Ansa, and Zared. Zared and Ansa were reaching out for me pulling on me with their deep claws cutting into my arms. Deni, my mother and my classmates were bound in chains being dragged around by their necks. Doing whatever Cypher tells them to do.

"No! Please no! Someone please help me" As soon as I said that I saw this white light coming towards me and I couldn't help but try to reach for it. As soon as I did I felt someone step on my foot, I couldn't help but to look up, it was me. I stopped myself from reaching that light.

———————•◆•———————

"Clear, we are losing her."

"Hit her again!"

"Clear!"

One sound kept beeping all around. The echo of that single ring seemed to grow and there was nothing that was going to change that tune. It was like those static noises that you tried so hard to get rid of when listening to the radio.

"Okay, I am calling it."

———————•◆•———————

"Yes, finally!" That demonic voice gloating in victory.

"No please, I am still here."

"Scream all you want no one can hear you." I saw this figure coming out of the light and what seemed like a fiery sword pierced through my own heart, causing this demonic version of me to burn to ashes. I was able to reach up towards that light again, to that figure, calling for help.

———◆———

"Wait doctor, I am detecting a heartbeat."

———◆———

"What?! No!! She is mine to torment for all eternity!" That white lighted figure proceeded to come over towards me. Burning the ones who were digging their claws into me. His presence caused them to let go of me immediately, completely terrified; running away as fast as they could. Cypher, who didn't dare to approach the light, was completely filled with rage.

"She doesn't belong to you, she has chosen me." That figure took the sword he had and cut the chains that Cypher had in his hands that were tied around my legs getting ready to drag me in. Cypher, being defeated, disappears, blending into the darkness. This figure picks me up and carries me into the light. I couldn't help but smell this pleasing aroma. There were no better words to describe this scent; all I could say is that it was sweet like honey and as bold as a lion.

———◆———

"Paulina? Can you hear me?" My eyes started to adjust while I was having trouble waking up. "Welcome back Ms. Saville, that was a close call. Can you tell me your name, date of birth and age?"

"Paulina Saville and November 17th, 2004."

"And your age?"

"I am 19 years old. What happened? Where am I?"

"You were in a coma, you also died. And you are here in Colorado."

"Colorado?"

Chapter SEVENTEEN

"WELL GOOD MORNING Ms. Saville, I am…"

"Doctor Arlo."

"Umm, well yes. You seemed to have some sort of traumatic fall. You had experienced a broken leg, an injury to your left eye and multiple scratches on your arms, very deep cuts. Police have ruled it out as either an animal attack or the tree branches being stuck to you as you were rolling down the hill. Unless you can remember anything about that night."

"Exactly what night doctor? What is today's date?"

"March 15th, 2023"

"That is impossible, I was supposed to be here from the 28th to the 4th. I was still in D.C."

"Paulina, you have been here in Colorado since your winter break. You have been in a coma for 2 and a half months. You had an accident on New Year's Day."

"I know that I had an accident on New Year's Day, and I was here in the hospital for a few weeks, and then I was free to go back to my mother's for a couple weeks, and I was back in D.C and I was suppose to come back to Colorado for a check up with you, plus visit my mother and even Ethan."

"I am sorry Paulina, none of that happened. There is a possibility you were dreaming."

"It was so real though, I was living my life after my injury."

"Well, people have mentioned that they entered into an outerworld while dreaming in a coma. Perhaps that is where you were."

I walk out of the hospital doors all over again, thinking about everything that I dreamt about. As I am waiting for my Uber, I see a familiar black car pull up. The door slowly opens and my heart starts running a marathon. A tall handsome stranger gets out.

"Ms. Paulina, welcome back."

"Ethan!" I ran and jumped on him. He was the only one I wanted to see. He grabs me and holds me tight. Tears rushing down my face.

"I missed you too. Are you ready to leave, your mother is expecting you, she would have come with me to pick you up but she wanted to make sure your room was ready. Getting everything situated and comfortable for you."

"Thank you, for being here and picking me up."

"Anything for you," he gives me the warmest smile. I couldn't help but take a whiff of his cologne as I was starting to let go of him. He walks around to place my bags in the trunk. He smelled super sweet and it had its touch of strong masculinity.

"Sweet like honey, bold as a lion."

"Paulina did you say something?"

"Your cologne, it smells sweet like honey and is as bold as a lion, if I were to describe it. What is it called?"

"Oh, it was a gift, it is called 'Samson' why is it okay."

I smiled and tears of joy could not be held back. Ethan was the one who saved me in my dream. "Everything is more than okay." As I got into the car Ethan shut the door, for the first time I felt that I was no longer trapped behind this door, I felt like I was being sealed into a place of protection.

We finally made it back to my mother's house. She comes running out with her arms wide open. "Darling, welcome home! Please come in, come in. Ethan, do you mind getting her bags please and taking them upstairs, it would be much appreciated."

"Of course ma'am," he says with a polite and respectful smile. I turn around and look at him, he looks up, giving me a wink.

"I have made up your bed and room, tonight we are going to have a special guest for dinner. I want you to join us, I have some very special news."

Still scared of what I saw in my dream when it comes to my mother, the way she helped torment me, I didn't know how I felt. It was just a dream after all, right? "Uh, yeah; sure mom. What time should I be ready?"

"Dinner is at 7. So you have plenty of time to rest and get ready."

"Yes, plus I need to contact my professors and see if there is anything that can be done for make- up work."

"I contacted your teacher's while you were in the hospital. Most of your classes had to drop you, honey. Your diagnosis wasn't a guarantee of your return."

"Oh okay. I guess I will have to take those classes in the fall."

"Well there were two remaining classes that said if miraculously you woke up before the end of the school year, if you pass their final essay's or presentations then you will get the credit you need for your transcript."

"Do you happen to remember what their names were?"

"Professor Dana and Professor Cypher. That Professor Cypher is something else though, he said that your presentation needed to be given on the 21st."

"Of this month?!"

"Yeah, I guess you have to re-take that class, it is tomorrow, there is no way that you can make your presentation."

"Did he tell you what it is I had to present?"

"Yeah I wrote it upstairs on your desk." I ran up the stairs to get the sticky note. What a crazy coincidence it was the same presentation I needed to give in my dream. How could this be, I was terrified to fail his class, most of all I was terrified to re-take that class again. I wanted nothing to do with Cypher after that dream. It was way too real to think it was only a dream.

"Knock, knock. May I come in?"

"Of course Ethan. Hi."

"Are you okay?"

"Not really, I am supposed to give my final presentation and it is due tomorrow. It determines if I fail or pass, and I am not trying to fail. I need to put together a presentation talking about what this class has done for me and why I would recommend it to others. And apparently he grades it very difficult, there are no grading checklist recommendations that allow us to know what we need to have."

"Well it is an opinion based presentation, it can't be that bad can it?"

"I don't know, a couple of classmates who have been there for three years have just failed over and over again."

"Wow, crazy. Well looks like there is nothing you can really do, the 21st is tomorrow. So with that let's focus on today. It has enough problems of its own. Why worry about tomorrow, it hasn't even come yet." Why does everything he says bring me so much peace? "Plus, how about we work on that presentation and when you return back to school you go into his class demanding to give your presentation, don't take no for an answer."

"I can do that?"

"Yes, I will even be there with you, if you want."

"Really? I would love that." I get up out of my chair and wrap my arms around his neck and give him the biggest kiss I believe I possessed.

"I am glad our feelings are mutual." Smiling from ear to ear. "I love you Paulina."

"I love you Ethan!" After I said those words I can hear the sound of love falling into this place, a harmony that only two people who are in love with one another can obtain. It was as if Heaven met Earth and there was a beautiful melody that was all around us. A bond that was not easily broken.

"Paulina, are you ready? Our dinner guest will be here any moment now. Please come down."

"Coming mother," I head down the stairs and I see my mom checking out her hair and make-up by the front door mirror. "Mhmm," I cleared my throat to get her attention."

"Wow, you look beautiful, honey."

"Mom, there is something I want to say, oddly enough it feels like I am saying it again."

"What do you mean?"

"Nothing, really. Anyways I am sorry for what happened at the Christmas party. What I did was completely out of line and I didn't mean to cost you your career."

"Paulina, it is okay. That is under the bridge. When you got into that horrible accident I realized that nothing else mattered, definitely not holding a grudge from that stupid argument. I know that you didn't intentionally do it." We embraced in a long and tearful hug. "Oh, no my mascara. I should clean my face haha. I will run down the hall real quick to clean this up."

"Haha, I guess I will use this mirror then."

Ding Dong

"Our guest is here sweetie, can you please get that."

"Sure mom," I opened the door and what do you know it was Mrs. Jones.

"Paulina, how lovely to see you!"

"Mrs., Mrs. Jones; you are here?"

"Yes, your mother invited me, may I come in?"

"Oh, uh, please do."

"Thank you. Where is your mother?"

"She is..."

"Right here Patricia!" She says coming down the hall extending her arms like an eagle giving off a welcoming signal, assuring she wanted a hug.

"So good to see you."

"Yes, indeed. Paulina I am sure you are curious as to why she is here. Well a few days after the whole Christmas party incident Patricia reached out apologizing for the way she acted towards me. Not only that, she told me how many people raved about the event. I am now officially a business woman who owns her own event party planning business! Isn't that great!?"

"Wow, mom, that is amazing!"

"Yes, so Patricia here has been my partner on this journey and once a week we have a celebratory dinner. I hosted it here this evening instead of going to her restaurant, Cerchio." She says while taking a sip from her champagne glass.

"Isn't that Mr. Jones' restaurant?"

"Not anymore, I am now a divorced woman. I got tired of the unfaithfulness we had in our marriage. That is not something I ever planned for my life. Since we both were unfaithful we decided to split everything down the middle."

"Oh, okay. When did this happen?"

"Not long after the Christmas party, your mom and I went on a trip for a couple weeks to get our heads on right. I needed some time away from him. That really helped me to make my decision."

"Okay..."

"Thank you Paulina, for helping me see straight. Thank you Eva for your friendship, cheers!"

"Cheers!" My mom clings her glass.

"Cheers," I follow right behind.

Chapter EIGHTEEN

"ETHAN, WHERE ARE you taking me?"

"Well it's called a surprise for a reason, it's not supposed to be predictable. Plus we are almost there."

"Fine, you won't let me run into anything, right? I can't see out of this blind fold."

"Once again, that is the point of it. Do you trust me?"

"Yes, I do."

"Then okay, just know that I have you. Always." He is still holding on to my hand leading me to what seemed like the great outdoors. I could feel a light breeze brush against my cheeks. "Okay, stop right here. On the count of three I am going to remove the blindfold and you can see your surprise. Okay?"

"Okay, now hurry and take it off, this is making me so nervous and excited all at once."

"Haha, okay. 1...2...3... here we are."

I couldn't help but stand still for a moment, taking in this fresh breath of air. If a scenery could ever be described, there would not be enough words to describe what I am seeing justice. The amount of work Ethan put into bringing all of this together; a picnic on top of a mountain. The view is spectacular, the little decorations he placed up all around us brings a smile and tears to my eyes. You can hear the sound of the river not too far off. How relaxing and peaceful of the wind blowing freely from any direction it chooses. As I am taking in this wonderful and thought out moment, time couldn't get any more perfect than this; can it? Ethan starts to hug me from behind, living in this moment with me. Staying quiet and engaging to wait on my next move. "This is absolutely breathtaking and yet at the same time I feel like I am breathing for the very first time."

"I am glad you like it," his head facing towards me waiting for me to give him permission to kiss me.

"I love it," I say, turning to face him. "Like I love you," leaning into him and kissing him. I turned into his chest grabbing his neck to ensure that I wanted him even closer to me. He grabs my waist pulling me in. If a kiss could seal the love and loyalty between two people, then let me tell you there was nothing going to break what we had sealed in our hearts.

He pushes me back to see my face, moving my hair from my cheek, staring into my eyes. He then grabs my hand and leads me to the table so we can sit and eat. A magnificent afternoon went by faster than I had expected. We needed to start taking down the decorations. "Hey, Paulina, do you mind putting the dishes in the picnic basket? I'll get everything else."

"Yeah, of course." I start collecting up the dishes and slowly put them in the picnic basket. I couldn't help but see a bulge sticking out of the inside pocket. I reached in there and I pulled out a jewelry case. I was curious to see what was in it. My eyes widened, it couldn't be. How is this even possible? My mother's ruby ring that Deni and I had lost when we were children. "Why do you have this? Where did you find it?" I turn around looking at Ethan eager to know the answers.

"Your mother gave it to me."

"That is bull, she wouldn't dare to do that. This is the ring my father gave her as his promise to her!"

"Paulina, please I wouldn't lie to you. Your mother found it while we were in the attic cleaning it out. This was when you were in a coma. She found it while moving some boxes around and as she saw it she started to cry. I ran to her and asked her what was wrong?"

"Did she tell you how she got mad at me for playing with it?"

"Yes, she did. She told me how awful she felt for treating you like that. How she was trying to deal with grief herself and she didn't know how to take care of you anymore. She was trying to get herself together and situated so you could have a successful upbringing. She knows that it doesn't excuse the way she has treated you. Maybe one day, if you are open to hearing her side, she can tell you about what she was going through and the things she had to do, the best way she knew how."

"Wow, I don't know what to say. That doesn't answer the question as to why you have it?"

He walks closer, smiling. He grabbed my hand and said, "Your mother has noticed how much you mean to me and she gave me this ring to symbolize the same promise your father made to her. I have carried it around waiting to make that same promise to you. I knew that if you saw the ring, that it would be so special and dear to you."

"You want to be my forever promise?"

273

He couldn't help but giggle, "There is no one else I'd rather be with. This isn't how I imagined doing this moment, yet I don't see a better time like the present time. Paulina, will you seal my devotion to you, my love for you, through the highs and lows by wearing this ring? Will you be my forever promise that I know you were always meant to be?"

Deeply looking into my eyes with compassion, my excitement overtook me and I said, "Yes!" He placed the ruby ring on my hand. I jump into his arms and I can't believe this man is real, right here just wanting to love me, ready to spend the rest of his life with me.

"Come on my love, let's get going." As I hop back into the truck, I was the happiest that I have felt in a really long time. I was looking out the window while driving down the mountain and as everything seemed to be moving at the same speed as us, I couldn't help but look out to the trees. The trees reminded me of that night, of that dream. I knew what I needed to do next, and I knew exactly who I wanted to be right by my side when I did.

"Ethan, can you take me to where my accident took place please."

We got down out of the truck, the sun may have been hiding behind the mountains, but I knew that if I followed through with this a greater light was going to break forth. I start feeling a tightening in my chest, trying to convince me that I won't find healing. Ethan must have known that I stopped in my tracks because he grabbed my hand, "Hey, I am here for you, we will keep going if you want to."

"Do you think I can find healing here?"

"Going back to the place that caused you trauma and pain is not only courageous, it also shows how this doesn't have to rule over your life anymore. If that isn't healing, then what is?"

"Thank you for being here with me."

"There is nowhere else I'd rather be."

We keep walking and there is the tree. I become hesitant like I made the

275

wrong choice. Then as I looked closer I saw a couple under the tree talking and kissing. To see something good, beautiful and genuine made the tree not so scary. Ethan waited patiently to follow my lead as to what I wanted to do next, I step forward, continuing my journey. Next thing I knew I was looking down at the pit where I was. At least I thought it was a pit, but it actually was a ditch. I made it, I am staring my trauma in the face. I started to yell and cry at the same time. I felt a sense of relief, there was a freedom being released, no longer being tormented, I was allowed to be someone new. Ethan comforted me in the only way he knew best. Him just being there, witnessing breakthroughs in my life was good enough for me. After being there for 10 minutes crying, with snot coming out of my nose, eyes all puffy, throat aching; feeling and looking like a hot mess. Ethan spoke very softly, "Here in this moment you never looked more beautiful."

"Ethan?" I lift my head up off his lap to look at him. "How did you know where to find me? Well in my dream while I was in a coma, you found me that, is what your father said anyways. Is that true, or is that just a scenario from my dream?"

"That night I did find you. When you hadn't texted me I got worried. So, I went looking for you. Your mom had told me before your flight landed that she left your "Find My Iphone" app on your phone, and you had yet to disable it. And this was for her to ensure you were okay no matter what, while at Georgetown and even here. Even when you left that night after the Christmas party she was checking to see where you were. She knew you were at a strip club and made sure you checked into a hotel safely. She gave me access so I could keep an eye on you until you left for Georgetown in case something were to happen if she was ever out of town for business. When I saw that you were practically in the middle of nowhere and just staying still, I knew something was wrong so I drove here as quickly as I could. I saw the blood and it led me to you. I saw you frozen cold in that ditch and I went down and grabbed you. I picked you up and put you in my car and drove you to the hospital as quickly as possible."

"My mother did all that? You did all that for me? After everything. I thought she hated me this whole time. Oh my, thank you, I am thankful for you and my mother. I wouldn't be here if it wasn't for either of you." I start to cry after coming to the realization of what my life has come to and how I could have missed out on so many memories and years if my mother who I thought hated me never kept tabs on me. Ethan holds me close.

"We never know who is behind the scenes wanting what's best for us or waiting for our doom to come. Eventually we will see who is trying to pull us closer to our best that is yet to come or pulling us down further away from where we are destined and called to be. This comes eventually when revelation is brought forth and we are willing to see the truth that is brought before us. This all happens in its proper time.

"Speaking of things coming to the light, can I share with you the dream that I had?"

"Please do."

I tell Ethan every detail of my dream and how real it felt. He listens and is intrigued, really focused and paying attention to everything I have to say. What a wonderful listener he is.

"Well, what do you think?"

"That is a very intense dream, there are some similarities to reality and the dream. It seems that in the dream and in real life before the accident you were drinking, partying, running away, and having lust on your mind. I believe your torment is from what you allowed in, the doors you opened."

"Opened?"

"Yeah, you know what a torture chamber is meant for. It is usually hidden away and behind a door. Now those who go into a torture chamber are those who have committed a crime, or they have valuable information, or even valuable themselves. Torture is a way to cause someone to slowly die; no remorse, no rest. Complete horror and despair. The legance you were willing to make with your professor opened that door. The way he would treat you like you were nothing, the way your friends would say horrible things about you and betray you. You felt like this was the good life, this was the best it was going to get, you practically were willing to tell him you love him. Those were the words he wanted to hear. Because you were about to die without the knowledge of what true love really was, he would be able to have you forever because that is all you ever knew. You would keep being tormented by him and his mocking would never cease."

"Why was my mother, Deni and my classmates in chains though?"

"Perhaps because they got caught up in their own similar open doors, you have to be the one to help them see the light."

"Why was I stepping on myself?"

"I believe that part symbolizes how you were causing yourself to die too, you accepted all of the anger, hurt, and lack of self-worth without trying to really see and find a resolution."

"In my dream the light was you, I am to lead them to you?"

"You lead them to true love. Love is patient, kind, and forgiving. Share the way I have treated you with them. It isn't about them deserving any of it, it is simply a free gift to give. If we really love those we say we do, then there can not be conditions. Love doesn't come with any. That is why I will never say I love you because and add a bunch of conditions to it because if you stop meeting those conditions then I would stop loving you and you would feel the pressure that you could never gain my love back or try your absolute hardest to. For example I could say I love you because of the way your hair blows in the wind, you clean the house, or how you take care of yourself. The wind will stop blowing at some point, the house won't be clean one day, and health fluctuates."

"Okay, I get it."

"I love you for you. I choose to love you."

"Thank you Ethan." I lay in his arms. Time was non-existent right now. Then a light bulb went off in my head, "Oh my goodness, I know now what I need to do. I need to get back to Georgetown!"

Chapter NINETEEN

"THANK YOU MOM for everything, for listening to me and for willing to share your side with me."

"I am glad that we were able to clear the air, I am sorry that you felt this way all these years, not realizing that you were bottling all of this up. Now that I look back at all of this I feel so horrible for how I treated you..." my mom starts to choke up, pride trying to hold back the tears. I grab my mom's hand signifying that it is okay to let it out. She got that message alright because her tears came like a flood.

"Mama, you are not horrible, just because some of the things seem to be horrible doesn't make you a horrible person. Hearing from your perspective I can see now how you were trying to do the best you could, not realizing how it would affect you or me, until now." She grabs onto me as if she was holding onto a rope that potentially was to save her life if she were to be hanging over a cliff. There were more tears shedding here than a desert finally getting a rain storm. After a while I get up from hearing a knock on the door. "That is Ethan. Mom, he is taking me back to Georgetown. I will be back for the Summer. Keep me updated on your business and how it is going. I can't wait to hear where you end up next."

"Okay sweetie, enjoy the rest of the semester, I will see you soon." One last hug is given and her phone rings.

"Go ahead and take it mama," I grab my bags and start to walk away. Just before she answers the phone I turn around and say to her, "I love you mom and I always will." The look on her face felt relieved. Her posture seemed to straighten out as if she was free from the weight and burden she had been carrying for so many years.

"I love you too Paulina," her smile breaking through like how the sunlight breaks through the clouds after it rains.

Opening up the door Ethan is standing there patiently waiting for me. "Are you ready to head over to the airport?"

"Yes, I need to do this now. The sooner the better."

"Okay, well right this way my lady." He chuckles, extending his arm for me to grab onto. I couldn't help but laugh with him and grab his arm. Getting into the car I was trying to mentally prepare myself for what was to come. I was technically a week late from my assignment for Cypher's class. How does he grade? I was going to demand that he listened to my presentation no matter what. I was not going to be in his class ever again.

"Gate 107 now boarding, gate 107 now boarding. If you can please make your way over that will be fantastic!" Why did I feel so nervous, the last time I was on a plane I had that fowl, tormenting dream. I felt weak in my knees, standing still in the line. I couldn't move. The images coming back up, the thought of Cypher was freezing and shutting down every nerve.

"Hey lady! Are you going to move or what? Some of us will like to get on our flight today."

"Leave her alone, can't you see she seems a little bit scared. Let her catch her breath."

"Why fly if you are scared then, we don't have time for this!"

"Honey, are you okay? Do we need to call someone for you?" I shake my head, that was the only thing that I could do. Words were non-existent, not even sounds seemed to ever be invented.

"My love, I am here. I got you!" Ethan comes pushing through the crowds. I look over at him starting to lift myself up a bit. "I am sorry I was running late, I had to stop at the gift shop to get this for you." He held up a deer stuffed animal, handing it over to me. I grab it and he wraps his arms around me. Bringing me closer to him, he whispers in my ear, "I saw you struggling and could hear your heart calling for help so I came as quickly as I could. I am always here for you, forever I will stay by your side."

"Yesterday and forever I vow I will." We head into the plane taking our seats. He seemed to make the images and words that were flashing in my head go from roaring to not ever being there. Nothing could challenge his presence when he steps into the room. This flight seemed so quick. The time I was spending with Ethan seemed more like seconds. Time just seemed to be a word.

"Thank you for choosing Lighthouse Airlines, if you don't mind exiting in an orderly fashion one row at a time that would be much appreciated. We hope that you enjoyed your flight as much as we enjoyed your company."

"Are you ready to step foot onto your new journey?" I guess I never thought of this being a new journey. Mainly because

I have already been here before. When actually listening to those words I knew that he wasn't wrong. This was a new journey because of the revelation I had been given. Stepping onto a territory that I needed to possess and overtake, not for my sake but for the sake of freeing others.

"Where are we off to?"

"Well my class isn't until tomorrow morning, so we have the rest of today to spend with each other. First thing first though," I give him this crazed look. Ethan is preparing himself for what is about to come

next from my mouth. "Food!" I scream in the middle of the airport, dancing in circles. He starts laughing at me; he dances with me, spinning me around.

"Let's go get you some food my love."

"I want to take you to this restaurant I have dreamt about trying since the moment I got here. I just never had a chance."

"After you," he moves his arm to make way for me to walk in front of him.

"Whatever your heart desires." We get into our Uber and make our way to Ahava.

"Wow! I can't believe we are here. This is so exciting!"

"Welcome to Ahava, how many will be included in your party today?"

"Just two ma'am and may we please have an outdoor table, it seems like a beautiful day and it should be shared in the same light as this beautiful young lady here."

"Of course sir," she smiles and starts walking. "Right this way please."

"You really know how to make me smile and feel like the only woman in the world for you." He smiles and takes hold of my hand, confirming that I am. For the next couple of hours we were eating and talking. Enjoying the luxurious moment. Not to say this was a high class restaurant, but it sure felt like it, with the attention and catering we were getting. "I have a couple more places I would really like to go to. Let me just say that I planned out a day for us."

"Haha, I knew you might have. You lead the way, I am excited to see what else you have planned."

"Perfect! Well we must get going then." Leaving the restaurant I ended up running into someone I didn't think I would. "Nick?!"

"Lina?! Where have you been? Kind of been missing you around the parties lately, among many other things," he says winking at me trying to take hold of my hand. I quickly removed my hand from him. "What's all the hostility, I should be the one giving you that, after all you did just ghost me."

"Yeah about that Nick..."

"Hey, are you ready to go?" Ethan comes out of the restaurant grabbing my lower back and notices Nick and I. "I am sorry, I didn't mean to interrupt."

"Oh so this is why I haven't heard from you. Got yourself a new toy to mess around with. Take it from me man, don't even bother. She is not even worth it." Nick was furious and scowled me down.

Like I was the biggest enemy he had ever known. Instead of stabbing him in the back, the look he gave was more like I stabbed him in the heart.

"Excuse me, you will not talk about her like that. Paulina is worth everything to me..."

"Nick, I am so sorry. I didn't mean to hurt you."

"No you just meant to sleep with me whenever you felt like it and disposed of me like I was tissue. Because that is all anyone is to you, disposable. I thought that those rumors were just lies. Seems like they were true." Nick scowls at me then walks away, not ever looking back. I couldn't help but to feel shame come crashing over me. One moment you are walking on water, just going with the flow and then out of nowhere the winds pick up and waves just get bigger and bigger all around you, making its mission to overtake you. I started to dart towards any direction, that was going to get me out of that circle that trapped me.

"Paulina!" I can hear Ethan calling out to me. "Paulina!" But the further I ran away the less I could hear his voice in the distance. I ended up at the bottom of Chain Bridge. Completely in shock, not realizing that my hurt and pain had caused someone else to be hurt and feel pain. I didn't realize through my careless actions and words that they could either lift someone up or tear them down. 'Accountability' kept popping into my head. I never meant to hurt Nick or anyone else, intentionally. I thought about everyone else I might have ghosted all because I was afraid to show anyone my true self. Looking into the water, what is my true self? Who am I? I am here thinking about all the ones I have wronged, not really asking for it, or knowing that this is what they were going to get from me. How can I make any of it right? I look up towards the sky letting the sunlight hit my face. I take a deep breath, as soon as I open my eyes I can see Ethan at the top of the bridge, looking at me. Waiting for me to go to him. Oh Ethan, he can't ever seem to get a break from witnessing my mess ups. He does not deserve this, I would understand if he just wanted to call it quits on me. Knowing me, I would. After a few more minutes I get up and go to Ethan, he doesn't say a word the whole time I am walking up. As I finally look up to see if he is still there, I can't help but see that his arms are extended out for me to run to. I cry and book it into his arms, afraid that he would change his mind. When holding me I knew right then and there he wasn't ever going to change his mind about me. "You are my reason," that is all he said as I just buried my face into his arms.

We ended up continuing the rest of the day after that fiasco. I took him to the art gallery and we walked around Anacostia. Eating ice cream and enjoying the day as if nothing had happened. I believe he was waiting for me to be willing to share with him the issue. We took a seat on a nearby bench. I finally was ready to face the elephant in the room. "Ethan?"

"Yes Paulina."

"I want you to know that the person who I was when I was with Nick is not who I want to ever be again. You are not a play toy, neither was he or anyone else I took for granted in my life," starting to let out some tears I struggled to continue to say, "please don't judge me based on the person I was. I can't ever say that you won't run into a few demons of mine from the past or even current that I am not fully aware of. Please continue to stay by my side, like I will continue to hold onto you."

"Paulina, I am not oblivious to the fact that you don't have a past, I know you do. My decision and choice in loving you and wanting to be with you is not based on what you have done, what you are even doing now, or will ever do. Just don't keep running away when something from your past comes up, don't run away from me.

I want to be there for you, to help you get through it."

The next morning came, it was time to head over to Cypher's class and to finish this once and for all. After the experiences I have had and the way Ethan has come into my life the way he did, how can I not be thankful to be on this side of the grave. After Ethan and I had an in depth conversation last night, he gave me a kiss goodnight and walked me to my dorm room. I didn't want the night to end there, he was so considerate of my time and that I needed to get my rest for today, he left to go to his hotel room and told me he will be by my side during this presentation. Getting ready for the day, I drank a protein shake, I didn't feel like having anything crazy big, speaking in public is not my thing, I don't need to show the whole class how nervous I am. There was still no sign of Ethan anywhere and I needed to get to the classroom around the corner. I was standing in front of the doors, nervous to turn the door knob. This was now or never. I took a deep breath and swung open the doors. I entered and Cypher was sitting at the edge of his desk, and began to look up at me, turning away from his book.

"Well, well, well, look who is here? Miss Lina, please take a seat. My class is about to get started," he says while shutting his book at the same time the door closes behind me.

"I will not be taking a seat," as those words left my mouth a bunch of eyes and whispers filled the void of the room, but still left me feeling completely alone. "I have my presentation to give."

"Excuse me," Cypher says, filled with anger as if his eyes just turned red, his nose flaring up. "You are late for your presentation, you can not give it. As far as I am concerned you have failed and will be taking this class over again," he gets up off the desk and heads towards the whiteboard. I look around the room and notice Dillon and Rebecca slumping in their seats completely defeated. "Now once again, take your seat." Those words made me feel like I was powerless. I didn't let that stop me from continuing to examine the classroom. I finally saw it for what it really was, seeing people who felt hopeless and had no faith in their future. People who felt like a bunch of failures with no redemption. Life completely drained from each and everyone of them. Being tortured day in and day out. Trying to obtain success in their own lives, over their own demons but they didn't know how. They just did what they were taught to do by the influences that they have encountered since they were children to now. I couldn't help but look over at Deni lost and confused, forgetting who she really is. Zared and Ansa smiling as if they had won, walking over to Cypher and grabbing onto him as if they were proud to be on his side. Next thing I knew the classroom doors swung open behind me, I looked back and I saw Ethan standing in the doorway as a beam of light was finally shining in this room.

At that moment I knew I could stand up to Cypher. I turned back around to look at all of them quivering at the edge of the desk. "I am going to give this presentation. This class has done nothing for me but tormented me from the moment I got here. Questioning my worth, seeking after myself, afraid of what others thought of me, trying to continually please people, being a consistent failure and feeling like I am a victim. Dragging others down with me because I didn't want to get better, to do better. This class has clogged up my memory, spread lies and division. You Cypher had tried to color this room by making this presentation about the subject of this class and knowledge. When all you were doing was being deceitful and manipulating us, to hide us from the truth. The truth is that you want us stuck in here with you, misery loves company. The fact that you know how valuable and precious we are, is art. The psychological part is to see what triggers us, to expose that and use it against us as if we could never amount to anything more or even great. One thing that you have hoped for us to never encounter was the power of love. Love goes against everything you have tried to play here. Failure, depression, anxiety, and not being enough to encounter anything good. To come to know love that is freely given shows hope that we can win and obtain something so beautiful. That there is a future for someone like me in this world. Being worthy or having self-worth, to know love confirms to me that I was not created by accident, that I do have a purpose despite my flaws and the wrong decisions I have made. You tried all year to cover our eyes with this filth and darkness to keep us from really seeing and accepting love given to us, within us. The way you have been distracting us to believe that it is all about an opinionated assignment when in fact it is much bigger. Just like a magic trick, we are shown that this is an illusion when we are actually being deceived because the main trick is happening somewhere else. To you love is a cancer, when in reality love is the remedy. My lustful desire that had taken over all year long kept me from knowing love. This man, right here has shown me that there is such a thing as love, that it is not just a word or just a feeling. It is an action; a choice. Just like you have placed into Dillon's mind that he will always be a failure and wouldn't amount up to anything so why bother trying anymore and yet failure is not his fortune. Or how about Rebecca, you have poisoned her mind that she questions who she is, she is a beautiful woman who has been created fearfully and wonderfully."

Cypher stands up tall and starts talking, "What if you still choose what you have grown up to know your whole life? That way of thinking and doing things that you find to be comfortable to you starts to reel you back because the shift of perspective is too much to bear and makes you feel like you are more crazy than sane. You can point out this whole plan of mine all you want, even point out the things that other people face, does not change the fact of one thing still remaining," he looks confident as if he were about to challenge me and win. "One question remains here just for you though Lina," I was beginning to feel nervous. What did he have up his sleeve this time? I felt as if whatever my answer was going to be was going to determine how I move forward from this place. "Do you love him?" Cypher nods his way in the direction where Ethan stood.

I look back at Ethan, remembering everything that was shown to me about him and I, my mom, Deni, and even Cypher. Keep walking with Ethan on this journey wasn't going to be easy, and yet I felt secure that I knew I would be walking with him and that is all that mattered. He knew practically everything about me. Yes, the things he said cut me in a way that made me uncomfortable. Not to hurt me, but to shed me from my old self into something new, something beautiful.

Like a sculptor, cutting away the extra pieces not needed, engraving the marks that enhanced the artworks of beauty to make it unique among all others. Was I willing to make such a sacrifice, to know I don't always know what is best for me and getting placed into uncomfortable situations that diminished my pride and ego? Was I willing to be receptive to something I barely started to know for myself... I slowly looked down as I was thinking about everything I could be giving up. Did I really believe that true love conquers all? Having to choose once and for all to love Ethan and not just say that I do. I turned back around to see Cypher grinning from ear to ear, celebrating his victory. I stood up even taller and his smile was no longer existent, confused as to what was to come next. "I love Ethan with everything I have inside of me. You can't manipulate me any longer, clouding my judgment on love. I am willing to do all that it takes to prove my love to him, as he has done for me."

"No!" Cypher screams out in anger while Zared and Ansa are screaming in anguish. "Fine! Leave, but don't you think for one second that our voices won't keep lingering around in your head from time to time. I can play a long game just to see if you would give up on your 'so called love'."

"Watch me keep going without either of you to lean on." Immediately the three of them backed into the corner as if they were bound and stuck there.

"Leave us!" Zared screamed.

I step onto Cypher's desk declaring, "Everyone, you don't have to be here forever..."

"What are you doing? Stop that!" Ansa pleaded.

"I care enough about all of you, to be free from the mental, emotional, and spiritual beating that has been placed upon you guys to hurt yourself or even others. Stop! Do yourself no harm, any longer! I know what love has done for me, I know that love can free you too, despite everything that has ever been done to you or even what you have done to others, even yourselves. Don't let the lies of what Cypher and his goons have pounded in your head to keep you locked up here with torment everyday. Making you doubt your existence, your beauty, your intelligence, even your unique qualities such as your gifts. Don't even let the shame he has weighed on you stop you from thinking you aren't good enough. The most miraculous thing about love is that none of us are good enough and yet we all are freely given the opportunity to embrace something so wonderful. We all acquire peace and to feel accepted wholeheartedly. I know that starts with knowing love." I see Dillon start to pull himself out of the chair to stand up, then Rebecca, and many other classmates. I could almost hear the sound of velcro being separated from one another, feeling the struggle at first and the rest coming off easily.

"No! How dare you! Who do you think you are? I said you can leave, I never said anything about they could leave," Cypher is furious at this point.

"I am Paulina, a woman who is able to love because she has been loved. That just shows how much love has power over your ideology." The students who got up started to cry as they felt they were finally free, running out of the door and never looking back. I see Deni still in her chair, I get down off the desk and go to her. "Deni, get up. You don't have to live like this."

She looks at me as if I was the one who betrayed her. As if she couldn't recognize me. After she spoke these words my heart shattered, "I like who I am when I am with them, they treat me as if I am special, seen, heard; so how dare you come here and tell me what you think I need as if you know any better. I know who you really are."

"You don't know who I really am Deni, you only know of the person I was, people can change for the better, there is no crime in that. I only want what's best for you, you also have to see that for your-self too, just like I had to. They don't see you, you should feel special everyday of your life not only when you are opening up your legs. They don't hear you or see you, they are infatuated with what they can use you for."

"Leave me alone, I can't be associated with someone like you, someone who is all high and mighty."

"That is not what this is, Deni..."

"Go ahead and leave her, she will be fine in our hands, she made her choice," Cypher says while laughing. Looking around I still see half of the classroom staying in their seats, out of fear of the unknown. Even out of disbelief. I know I can't force anyone to make any decision out of their own free will but it doesn't hurt any less to know how they are hurting themselves and are okay with that.

"I won't stop loving you Deni and wanting what's best for you. I will be here when you decide to take a different route." I gave her a hug, even though she pushed me away. I showed her my tears that I cried specifically for her in hopes she would know and understand how sincere and genuine I was over her. That did nothing because all she could do was roll her eyes and stare to the front of the classroom. As I reached the top of the classroom amphitheater I was horrified by how many people didn't want to be free from this class and Cypher's grasp. So many people truly felt that they were trapped forever. That the thought of freedom is just an illusion. I know my work here isn't done. The doors may have closed behind me, I will continue to be here to lend an ear, an arm, or a voice to all of them when they come to wanting to know love. I have walked in similar shoes they had but I was going to walk in some new shoes.

Chapter TWENTY

Date: April 5th, 2023
History & Cycles Paper

PROFESSOR DANA YOU had asked us to write about what history I possess and what a loved one possesses. What makes me feel trapped? How can I break the cycle and how can we help others with the wisdom and knowledge that was presented to us? Well when this assignment was given to us at the beginning of the school year I had no idea what to write. I was also afraid to find out the answers to each and every question, basically of what was to come to the light and was I ready to face that harsh truth. I could just give you a bunch of fancy terms and a flattering story. I know I was only to give you a five page essay, but when it comes to what you wanted us to uncover, it is worth more than a simple five pages, this is my story of what I needed to go through. Needing to know my history of a traumatized past with my father passing away, my mother being a verbal abuser and abandoning my emotional needs. Which has led me to do the same thing, making it hard for me to connect with others and afraid of showing who I am. Sleeping around with guys not realizing that it was my way of coping like my mother did. I felt trapped in trying to keep up a persona with my so-called friends which was not even the real me, trapped in my own head filled with insecurity, lies, manipulation, and even doubt. Through my trial of self discovery, I have found the answer to it all. Now my story doesn't have a "everyone wins" ending, but it is a beginning to a greater journey that is to continue in my life. My story is to help others see what I have been shown. How can we say we really know someone, if we don't take the chance to hear or read their story; so here it goes. Hello, you don't know me and depending on who you ask, you will receive many different names such as, spoiled brat, ungrateful, funny, creative, kind, scandalous, mischievous, and even dead.

*P.S. I am Pauilina Saville, the journey to live on after trauma, torment and being bound to guilt, shame, and even fear is the continuing message. I hope you enjoyed the story of how love is the reason I'm here today, and the reason I will be against the teaching that comes from the **Classroom Around The Corner**.*

Thank You YHWH! You have shown me that I no longer need to be ashamed of my story because you have redeemed me from what was and have given me the hope to what is and can always be! (Jeremiah 29:11)

Thank You Mama!
Thank You Raheem!
Thank You Ray-Dizzle!
Thank You Mi Ultimo!

You all have played a special role in making this book happen. Truly a blessing and I will not ever forget it!

Much Love

Stand Firm

Many voices come and go,

Saying things that allow you to question what you think you know.

"What makes you think *He* loves you?"

Sometimes those voices come out of the blue.

Agreeing with their own question turning it around for a different view,

"Yeah, *He* would never love someone like you!"

That is when we stand firm,

Knowing that those lies can't make me doubt and squirm.

I know what *He* spoke over me and I affirm.

So my response to those demons that come on through,

"I know what *He* did to save me from you."